She pressed her face against his chest, and Lord help him, he wanted to stand there with her like that until she was no longer afraid.

"We now know that this threat is not idle. It's very real. I'm going to have twenty-four-hour surveillance at your place at the back and the front."

"But no one's there now."

"I'll call one of my guys as soon as we get in the vehicle. Your mother is going to be safe, Shayla. And so are you."

Looking up at him, Shayla nodded, and he could see the gratitude in her eyes. "I appreciate this so much. I promise I'll pay you."

"The only payment I want is you staying safe." Then Tavis gathered her in his arms and held her, feeling a sense of satisfaction as her body melted against his.

And maybe something else he didn't want to acknowledge.

COLD CASE SUSPECT

USA TODAY Bestselling Author

KAYLA PERRIN

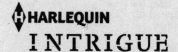

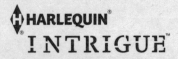

H HARLEQUIN®
INTRIGUE™

Recycling programs for this product may not exist in your area.

ISBN-13: 978-1-335-58215-7

Cold Case Suspect

Copyright © 2022 by Kayla Perrin

Harlequin Enterprises ULC
22 Adelaide St. West, 41st Floor
Toronto, Ontario M5H 4E3, Canada
www.Harlequin.com

Printed in U.S.A.

Kayla Perrin has been writing since the age of thirteen. She is a *USA TODAY* bestselling author of dozens of mainstream and romance novels and has been recognized for her talent, including having twice won the Romance Writers of America's Top Ten Favorite Books of the Year Award. She has also won the Career Achievement Award for Multicultural Romance from *RT Book Reviews*. Kayla lives with her daughter in Ontario, Canada. Visit her at www.authorkaylaperrin.com.

Books by Kayla Perrin

Harlequin Intrigue

Cold Case Suspect

Harlequin Kimani Romance

Taste of Desire
Always in My Heart
Surrender My Heart
Heart to Heart
Until Now
Burning Desire
Flames of Passion
Passion Ignited
Sizzling Desire

Visit the Author Profile page at Harlequin.com.

Chapter One

Shayla Phillips gripped the steering wheel harder, wondering if the black SUV behind her was actually following her.

You can't escape what you did forever. If you dare to show your face in Sheridan Falls again, you're going to DIE. It's time you pay for what you did!

The email threat she'd received just last week was permanently etched in her mind. She knew that returning home to Sheridan Falls posed a risk. But surely no one would know that she was heading to Sheridan Falls *right now*, would they? She had driven up the east coast from South Florida and was now heading west along the I-90. She was close enough to home that she *could* be being followed, even though that was unlikely. But the black SUV had been behind her for at least ten minutes, and that was making her wary.

Was it someone from her past who had noticed the Florida license plate? Someone who knew that she was heading back home because of her mother's illness? Or was she being exceptionally paranoid, seeing a threat where there wasn't one?

Stop freaking out, she told herself, drawing in a deep, steadying breath. *Of course you're being paranoid. No one from Sheridan Falls could know where you are right now.*

Returning her gaze to the road in front of her, Shayla saw the sign indicating that she was entering the city limits. The ominous message she'd received via her store's email had her tightening her grip on the steering wheel again. Was she risking her life by returning to the town where she'd grown up? Or was the message—like so many others sent to her over the past nine years—one simply meant to rile her? Make her emotionally suffer for the perceived wrongs she had done?

Shayla couldn't be sure. She only knew that returning to Sheridan Falls was the last thing she wanted to do, but given her mother's grave health diagnosis, she had no choice.

It had been eight and a half years since she'd left, but the familiar landscape was etched into her memory. The sprawling farmers' fields on the left side of the interstate. The thicket of trees on the right. Within ten minutes, she'd be in the center of town.

The memories of the long-ago night that Shayla had hoped to forget came flooding back. How she'd been on the verge of tears when she'd driven up to Lucas Carr's house. How angry Hayley had been at her. Her decision to skip the party because she was in no mood to hang out anymore. Jonathan antsy, irritated at the bickering between her and Hayley, just wanting to get to the party already. Hayley throwing her an angry look over her shoulder as she'd jumped out of the car. Shayla driving off in a huff of steaming tears, both furious and hurt that her friend was still so upset about that stupid dance competition.

And then the next day came the unbelievable news that Hayley and Jonathan were both dead. Their bodies found in a field behind the high school. Two bullets silencing the young teenagers' lives forever.

Tears began to well in Shayla's eyes as they always did when she thought of that horrible day. "Stop. Don't go there. It wasn't your fault."

And it wasn't. She knew that. And yet no one believed her. Not after the news that she had dropped Hayley and Jonathan off at Lucas's place for the party and she herself hadn't attended. To anyone who'd heard the story, it was obvious that Shayla hadn't attended the party because she'd known that Lucas was going to kill Hayley. And why? Because Shayla and Hayley had been fighting over the regional dance competition. As if Shayla cared to lose her best friend over something stupid like that.

That was why she was even more hurt over the fact that Hayley had let the competition come between them. Hayley, consumed with jealousy, had been enraged that she hadn't secured a spot. What was Shayla supposed to do? It wasn't her fault that the judges had scored her higher. It wasn't her fault that Hayley had been nauseous that day. If Hayley had made the regionals and she hadn't, Shayla would have been happy for her. Disappointed over her own failure, yes, but not mad at a friend over something that neither of them could control.

It was absurd that Shayla would want to see her best friend killed over something so trivial, even if Hayley had been irrationally mad at her. But Lucas had had a reputation for being a bad boy, which was why he was living with his aunt and uncle in Sheridan Falls in the first place, and it had been easy for everyone to assume that Lucas had gone to the dramatic lengths of murder to keep Shayla happy.

The rumors didn't have one ounce of truth to them, but the people of Sheridan Falls didn't care to see things sensibly. Some people loved small towns, but Shayla hated them. Hated that, no matter where she went, someone was looking at her. No matter what she said in her own defense, people believed what they wanted to. In coffee shops and on street corners everywhere, she had been the topic of discussion after the murders—with the theories about her taking a worse turn every time the story was retold.

Shayla hadn't even been able to grieve the loss of her friend without the scorn of the people in Sheridan Falls. In a town where often the worst news of the day was who had burned their apple pie, a real-life double murder had consumed the townsfolk and they had come after her like piranhas devouring their prey.

Shayla glanced in the rearview mirror. The black SUV was still behind her. Maybe someone *was* following her?

She indicated and went into the right lane. So did the SUV.

Shayla's breathing began to accelerate. Surely no

one from Sheridan Falls would know where she was right now. Unless someone had happened upon her on the highway and seen her Florida plates. Everyone knew she'd moved to Florida. Dazzle Dance Designs, the store she'd set up there to sell dance costumes and accessories, had even been burned to the ground— by someone from her past, she was sure.

Shayla pressed her foot on the gas, accelerating as she neared her exit. The SUV behind her sped up as well.

"I'm in the right lane," she grumbled. "Just pass me already."

Shayla tried to see into the SUV's front window, but it was tinted and she couldn't see who was driving. She looked ahead just as she was coming up to the ramp for her exit, which she took faster than anticipated. She had to clutch the steering wheel and pump the brakes so that she didn't careen into the guardrail.

The SUV stayed on the highway.

Shayla exhaled sharply. What was wrong with her? Why had she let herself get so worked up? It didn't make sense that anyone would be following her. No one knew the time and the date that she was heading back to her hometown.

As she exited the off-ramp and onto Main Street, she looked out at the landscape. It had changed a little bit. On the left side of the road, there was now a strip mall where there'd once been a farmer's field. And beside it, a new restaurant, an all-day breakfast joint. It was a perfect spot to cater to hungry travelers and give them an opportunity to spend some money between the restaurant and the shops. On the right side of the road, there were still fields as far as the eye could see.

Shayla pulled her car into the restaurant's parking lot, which was her destination. Then she called her cousin, Deedee.

"Hey, Shayla," Deedee answered warmly. "Are you here?"

"Just got off the highway. I'm in the parking lot of 24-Hour Breakfast and More."

"Perfect. Oh, I see you. Come on in, cuz!"

A smile touched Shayla's lips as she gathered her purse and exited her vehicle. It had been years since she'd seen her cousin, and she was looking forward to giving her a big hug.

Deedee was waiting just inside the restaurant doors as Shayla entered. She hadn't aged a day in five years, but she'd put on probably ten pounds, giving her a more robust figure, especially for her five-foot-two-inch height. Her black hair was styled in thin braids and pulled into a bun high on her head. Deedee's complexion, a warm chestnut brown, was flawless. A bit of burgundy gloss and mascara was all the makeup she needed.

Her welcoming smile melted away the rest of the unease Shayla had been feeling about returning to Sheridan Falls.

"Shayla!"

Shayla walked into her cousin's open arms, and the two swayed their bodies as they hugged for several seconds.

"Five years," Shayla mused as they pulled apart. "I can't believe it's been that long."

"And you made me go to Miami in order to see you," Deedee chastised playfully.

Shayla glanced downward before meeting her cousin's eyes again. "And I appreciate that. I know you prefer to be a homebody."

Deedee was a nervous flyer, and generally freaked out when stepping out of her comfort zone. At amusement parks, she preferred to watch the shows and skip the rides—except the merry-go-round.

"It was a fun trip," Deedee said, "but, whew, if I never step foot on another plane again, it'll be too soon."

"After everything, you know that it was easier for me to stay away."

"I know," Deedee said softly.

"You could have come back to see me over the years," Shayla said. "Driven down, of course. I think you enjoyed yourself much more than you thought you would when you came to Florida." And, at least in Miami, no one was specifically watching her every move, waiting for a chance to hurt her...

"I did love visiting you in Miami, but there were too many people for me. Too much traffic. I felt claustrophobic."

"You liked the beach though, didn't you?"

Deedee nodded. "Yes, the Atlantic ocean was gorgeous. But the lake here is far more peaceful. Without the threat of sharks."

Shayla threw her head back and laughed. "You never fail to make me laugh."

Deedee had tried to make light of her fear over sharks, but Shayla had known that she wasn't joking. She remembered her cousin dipping her toes into the warm, blue waters of the ocean while eyeing the deeper waters with a hint of fear. "You promise I won't get eaten by a shark?" she'd asked.

While Shayla swam and enjoyed the water, Deedee had been far more cautious, and Shayla knew that she hadn't enjoyed the experience as much as she should. Most of the time, she preferred to stay on the beach, claiming she was happy just taking in some sun. Shayla knew that her cousin had let her fears get the best of her.

"Anyway, come on in." Deedee grabbed a menu. "Have a seat right here." She placed the menu at the first booth. The restaurant was about seventy percent filled. It was definitely in a great spot right off the highway, and no doubt did good business. That's why Deedee had invested in this property, after all.

"Can I grab you a coffee or a tea?"

"I'd love a coffee," Shayla answered. "Cream and sugar."

"I'll be right back."

Shayla glanced around the restaurant as she took a seat in the booth. Most of the faces she didn't recognize. But there were a few familiar ones. Tammy Taylor seated with John Hetrick. They'd been a couple in high school, and the toddler in the high chair beside them had Shayla realizing that Tammy and John must have gotten married.

Deedee returned with the cup of coffee, the sugar and creamers on the side. "Have you had a chance to check out the menu?"

"Gosh, not yet," Shayla said. "But I assume you have some sort of home fries and scrambled eggs?"

"That comes with three pancakes as well."

"Okay by me," Shayla told her. "I'll take the works."

"The works it is. You've gotten way too thin."

Deedee was right. Stress did that to a person.

As her cousin ambled away from the table again, Shayla looked in Tammy's direction. Saw that Tammy was staring at her. Shayla offered a small smile, but Tammy didn't return it.

Shayla looked away, then played with her phone to pass the time. She checked emails and then spent some time browsing social media. She sent a text to her mother to let her know that she'd be at her place very soon.

"Here you go!" Deedee said in a cheerful voice several minutes later.

Shayla looked up to see her cousin placing the plate of scrambled eggs, home fries and a stack of pancakes on the table. She would never be able to eat all of this, but she welcomed it nonetheless. "Thank you, Deedee. This looks and smells amazing."

Deedee slipped into the seat opposite her. "How do you feel being back?"

Shayla swallowed a mouthful of scrambled eggs before speaking. "Well, it feels strange. It's been so long. Like I'm a stranger, yet also at home." She lowered her voice and added, "I saw Tammy Taylor over there. I smiled at her, but she just gave me a stony look."

"I know people here have long memories, but I think everyone will calm down once they hear you're back. Tammy's probably more surprised than anything."

"You're probably right," Shayla agreed. "But you know I told you that I got that email from someone.

Basically threatening to harm me if I came back to Sheridan Falls. I assume it's someone who knows my mom is sick and would expect me to be returning."

Deedee's lips twisted with concern. "I'm sure it's just someone trying to be a pain in your butt."

"That's what I want to think but… It does give me pause. As I was heading to the Main Street exit, there was this black SUV that seemed to be following me. If I switched lanes, it switched lanes too. I literally started to panic. But then I got off at my exit and the black SUV kept going."

"See?" Deedee said, and reached across the table to squeeze her hand reassuringly. "It's just nerves. I understand, it's gotta be difficult being back here after so much time. And after…everything."

"Yeah." Shayla sipped her coffee. "I guess I'm just stressed about being back here, hoping that people still don't hate me as much as they did after Hayley and Jonathan were killed."

Deedee nodded. "You know, it does worry me that you still get threats after all this time. I was thinking about something, so hear me out. I think you should consider hiring a bodyguard."

Shayla chuckled, as if the idea were absurd. "A bodyguard?" She shook her head. "No."

"Like I said, hear me out. Tavis Saunders, you remember him?"

At the mention of his name, Shayla's heart stuttered. How could she forget Tavis? He had been three years her senior, and Shayla had been secretly crazy about him. Tall, beautiful brown complexion, a smile that could tempt any woman. Of course, he never looked at her as anything more than Hayley's friend—he'd been Hayley's older cousin. And after Hayley's death, he had hated her just like everyone else.

"Of course I remember him," Shayla said.

"Well, guess what? He's a bodyguard now. He used to be a cop for a bit, now he's got an agency where he protects people."

"Really?" That surprised Shayla. But she wasn't entirely sure why. He'd loved football. She'd assumed he might end up playing professionally or maybe coaching. But once she had left Sheridan Falls, she hadn't talked to him again or tried to find him online. Nor anyone else for that matter, except her few closest friends and her cousin.

"Yep," Deedee said. "So he's someone you know, he's from this town, so he knows the people, and I think you should hire him just to be on the safe side."

"I thought you just said you didn't think the threats were real."

"I want to believe they're not real. But why take any chances? With someone like Tavis, you can be protected twenty-four-seven."

The very thought made Shayla's pulse race. But with desire or fear? She remembered how she had run into Tavis's arms after the murders, hoping for comfort. And for a few glorious seconds, she had felt safe in his arms. But as he'd pulled apart from her, the look on his face had been unforgettable. Confusion, hurt and anger all mixed together. "People are saying you had something to do with this."

"What?" Shayla had been stunned to hear him say

that. "You know that's not true. How could you even say that? Hayley was my best friend."

"Where's Lucas?" he had asked. His expression had been hard. Unwavering.

"If I knew where Lucas was, I would tell you. But I really don't think he had anything to do with this."

"He just disappears after Hayley and Jonathan were at his party? Come on, you're his girlfriend. You have to know where he is. Please, do the right thing and tell me."

But Shayla hadn't, and no matter what she had said, Tavis hadn't believed her. Just like the rest of the townsfolk.

"No," Shayla said. "I'm definitely not hiring a bodyguard. Especially not Tavis."

"I don't think you should dismiss the idea, but obviously it's your choice."

Shayla nodded. Then Deedee rose from the table. "I'll let you eat your food. I'm going to make the rounds, check on the customers."

"Thanks again."

Deedee smiled at her. "Of course. You're family. I'm always here for you."

Her cousin's words reassured her and helped her feel better about being back in town. Shayla then dug into the meal in earnest, eating most of the scrambled eggs, the home fries and one of the pancakes. When she was finished, she was stuffed.

She was sipping the last of her coffee when she saw Tammy and John heading toward the exit with their son. Tammy definitely made eye contact with her, and once again Shayla offered her a smile.

"Shayla," Tammy said, her tone unreadable. "You're back in town."

"Yeah," Shayla said. "I'm not sure if you heard, but my mother is sick."

"Yeah, I did hear. I'm sorry about that."

Shayla felt the tension in her shoulders relaxing. Tammy was being cordial.

"Of course, the stress you put her through over the years certainly hasn't helped her health."

The words were like a dagger in Shayla's heart. She didn't even know how to respond.

"She's stronger than most women," Tammy went on. "I do hope she pulls through."

"Thank you," Shayla said, her tone clipped.

"I hope you don't plan on going to the vigil this week," Tammy continued. "If you have any respect for the victims' families, you'll stay away."

"Tammy, I'm not here to make anyone feel—"

Shayla's words died in her throat when she saw the swift action of Tammy's hand scooping up the water glass. And the next thing she knew, cold water was hitting her in the face.

Shayla gasped. She heard others in the restaurant do the same.

"You've hurt enough people in this town," Tammy said. "No one wants you back here."

"That's enough," John said to Tammy. "Let's go."

And then Tammy hustled through the door with John and their son, leaving Shayla sitting at the table, embarrassed and crushed.

Chapter Two

Deedee rushed over to Shayla's booth the moment Tammy and John stepped out of the restaurant. "Oh my goodness! Shayla, are you okay?"

Dabbing at her face with a paper napkin, Shayla looked up at her cousin. "Yeah. I'll live. I guess this is what I should have expected coming back to town. No one is going to be happy to see me."

Deedee passed her more napkins from the adjoining booth, then also began to wipe off the table. "*I'm* happy to see you. Your mother's going to be happy to see you. There are others who will be happy to see you too. Tammy was close with Hayley—she's never gotten over the murder."

"And I am the number one hated person when it comes to that." Sometimes it seemed as though people hated her more than they even did Lucas, the one who had committed the crimes.

Shayla blew out a frazzled breath then fiddled with a strand of her shoulder-length curly hair. It was wet now, and it would frizz, but at least she wasn't heading anywhere after this where she needed to look great. And if she could convince her mother to relocate for treatment, she wouldn't even have to stay in this town for long.

Deedee wiped off the seat on the opposite side of the booth, then slipped onto it. "Look, you might want to rethink hiring Tavis. I mean, I know Tammy didn't physically strike you, but if others are going to get any crazy ideas to come and accost you...I think that having Tavis around will be a good idea."

Shayla nodded, but didn't actually voice an agreement to the suggestion. She didn't need to tell her cousin that she could never hire Tavis. Maybe it was silly, but the crush that she'd had on him had been real, and the disappointment after he had seen her through the same lens as the other people in this town had been too hard to endure. Sure, that was a long time ago, but she didn't feel like spending day and night with a man who couldn't stand her.

And right now, she didn't want to have that discussion with Deedee. She wanted to get out of there and head to her mother's place. That was most important.

But she was curious about one thing. "Tammy mentioned something about a vigil?"

"Yeah, there's a vigil every year. Didn't I tell you that?"

"On the anniversary of the deaths," Shayla said. "Of course. In four days. I didn't realize the vigils were still happening now."

"People say they'll have the vigils every year until the killer is brought to justice."

What had happened to Lucas? Shayla wondered. If she knew where he was, she would serve him up on a silver platter so that everyone in the town could finally get the closure they wanted—herself included.

Four days from now would mark the nine-year anniversary of the murders. The date was forever etched in her mind. Beginning of June, right after the school year had ended. Everyone had been happy to start summer break, their last summer together before they would head off to college or other post-graduate pursuits. It had been a time of hope and promise that had been tragically cut short for all of them.

"People get together at the high school, send up balloons, hold candles. Pray." Deedee paused. "Don't think you have to go just because you're in town."

"Hayley was my best friend."

"But if someone's upset with you… And the first one you went to nine years ago didn't end well."

It hadn't, because Hayley's and Jonathan's families had accosted her for being there. Their words had been ugly, and they had ultimately forced her away.

Now, Shayla steeled her shoulders. So much she had endured. Tammy's unexpected assault had had her feeling sorry for herself for a moment and questioning why she'd come back. But she needed to remember that she had nothing to feel guilty for. She might not like being here, and the people of Sheridan Falls might not want her here, but she needed to hold her head high knowing that she'd had nothing to do with what had happened to Hayley and Jonathan. There was no need for her to slink away and hide.

"I'll see how I feel on the day," Shayla explained. "If I do go, I'll stay at the back of the crowd." She shrugged. "I don't know. What I do know is that I need to get to my mother right now. See how she's doing. It's been way too long."

"Of course," Deedee agreed. "Call me later."

In the car, Shayla had even more resolve to face this town with the guts she hadn't had when she'd run away. Maybe by running she'd given them all more fodder to talk about.

It had been easier to leave because she hadn't been able to grieve the loss of Hayley and Jonathan or even to process all that had happened under the scrutinizing eyes of everyone in Sheridan Falls. The judgment had been too much for her, so she had taken off when she could, built a life for herself somewhere else far away.

But had it been a life? She had thrown herself into work, had few friends and barely socialized. Except for one six-month relationship with Paul, the firefighter who'd gotten frustrated with her inability to open up, she had only dated a handful of times. She had always been too afraid to let anyone get close to her. And she'd constantly worried that someone would make good on any of the numerous threats on her life. So, for the first several months while she'd lived in Miami, she had looked over her shoulder everywhere she'd gone until she'd started to feel a modicum of peace and safety. The peace had lasted for a while—until the day her store had burned to the ground four years later.

She had adjusted, setting up a digital storefront, where she still moved a lot of product, not just in South Florida but across the country and even internationally. The world of dance was intense, with costumes and accessories in high demand. It was something she knew, so she'd found a way to make a living from it since she'd stopped competing after Hayley's death. She thought one day she could possibly coach, but she'd run even from that idea, preferring to live in her own small corner of the world where she felt she was safe.

As she headed to her mother's place, Shayla realized that the way she'd lived hadn't been much of a life at all.

She put those thoughts behind her as she neared Belmont Street. The street she had grown up on.

She turned right and, within moments, was at number fifteen. Her house. It would always be her house, wouldn't it? The place she grew up never ceased being home.

She exited the car, straightened her shoulders in case any neighbors were watching, and headed up the driveway and then the front steps. Though this was still technically her house, she rang the doorbell. The nurse was expecting her and it seemed better that she announce her presence rather than just use her key to get in.

Less than a minute later, the door opened. The dark-haired woman greeted Shayla with a warm smile, her blue eyes brightening. "You must be Shayla."

"And you must be Jennifer."

"I am," Jennifer said, holding the door open wide. She was wearing royal blue nursing scrubs that complemented her eyes.

Shayla stepped into the house. Her eyes roamed

over the place that had been her home for the first eighteen years of her life. Not much had changed. Her mother's sprawling houseplant was still growing along the wall, though its leaves and stems stretched farther now, over the piano. The sofas were the same, with the floral design that was outdated, but her mother had refreshed the ornament on the coffee table. It used to be home to a horse sculpture, but now there was a vase with fresh flowers. She wondered if that was the nurse's touch.

"How's my mother?" Shayla asked, sadness pulling at her heart. She wasn't looking forward to seeing her mother sick.

"She's awake now. This is the perfect time to go and see her."

Shayla nodded. "Thank you." She headed down the hallway, already knowing that her mother had been moved downstairs for her home care.

The main level den, having been converted to a bedroom to house her mother, made it more convenient to get her to the bathroom, and easier for the nursing staff in general.

The room looked completely different. There was a hospital-style bed on the far right, and some shelving set up on the left, where there were medical supplies, from what she could gather. The sofa was gone, but there was an armchair. The other belongings in the room had been put into boxes that were now placed against the back wall.

But Shayla quickly looked past all that and focused on her mother, whose eyes were closed. Had she fallen asleep?

She walked toward the bed quietly. "Mom?" she said softly. "Are you awake?"

Her mother's eyelids flitted open. And then a smile spread on her lips. Shayla's eyes moistened. Her mother had the same warm smile, but her body was much smaller than it used to be. It hurt to see her like this, knowing that cancer was ravaging her body.

Shayla stepped forward and took her mother's hands into hers. "Mom. I'm so sorry I haven't been here for you. Why didn't you tell me you were sick sooner?"

"I didn't want you to worry. I know you have your life in Miami."

"*You* are my life, Mom." Unfortunately, her mother had decided to keep her cancer diagnosis to herself. Maybe she'd been unable to face it, or maybe she'd thought she was protecting Shayla. But Shayla wished she'd learned about the colon cancer before it hit the fourth stage.

And before the cancer had spread to her liver and abdomen.

If only Mom had agreed to move to Miami with her. She knew her mother was stubborn, the type who believed that whatever was going to happen should happen. It didn't help that to some degree she was afraid of doctors. But she'd let her situation become too grave too quickly by ignoring the signs.

"How are you feeling?" Shayla asked her.

"I've been better." She closed her eyes as if in pain and then reopened them. "I'm getting meds for the pain. And you see I have an IV attached here for fluids. The nurse is taking good care of me."

Shayla didn't want to cry in front of her mother, but tears escaped her eyes nonetheless. She brushed them away. "I'm here now. Anything you need, I'm here. You're going to get through this. Okay? *We* are."

Her mother merely squeezed Shayla's hand tighter. Shayla didn't know how her mom felt about fighting. It had to have been devastating to have received a cancer diagnosis. And she'd heard that chemotherapy made you sicker before you got better. Did her mother believe she was going to pull through, or did she think this was the end?

Shayla could not, and would not, accept that this was the end for her mother. As long as she was here, she was going to fight and help Mom fight. Maybe what she needed was her daughter in her life to show her she had more to live for.

"I'm gonna get my stuff from the car, get settled in. But if you need me, let the nurse know. I'll be here for you anytime you want me. Always."

"I know, sweetheart. You go on and get your things and get settled in. We'll catch up a bit later."

As Shayla left the room, the tears hit her full force. Seeing her mother having lost at least twenty pounds was crushing. Her mom had always been strong, independent, and had raised her fearlessly when her father had abandoned them both. Life wasn't fair, that was for sure. But Shayla was going to do whatever it took to help her mother get through this. She refused to believe this was the end.

Jennifer was standing in the hallway, her arms

crossed over her chest and a sympathetic expression on her face.

"Thank you so much for being here for my mother," Shayla said. "I really appreciate it."

"No problem," Jennifer told her. "I'm happy to be here, happy to help."

"You must think I'm a bad daughter. I've been away for so long. But I didn't know the extent of what my mother was going through. I guess she wanted to protect me."

"That's exactly what she was doing. And I don't judge you. Your mother speaks so highly of you."

The words filled Shayla with pride. "That's nice to hear."

"Um," Jennifer hedged, "do you mind if I say something?"

"Sure. What's on your mind?"

"I know this might be a touchy subject, but I just wanted to say that from all of my interactions with you on the phone, and talking to your cousin and your mother, I don't believe that you had anything to do with what happened to your friend and her boyfriend nine years ago."

Somehow, Shayla managed to stop herself from reeling backward at the statement. That wasn't what she'd expected. The nurse didn't even know her. Why would she broach this topic?

"I'm sorry if I'm stepping out of line here, but this is a small town and everybody knows what happened. When I first got the job taking care of your mother, a couple of the neighbors talked to me and made me aware of what went on. And… I'm sorry, I've offended you."

"No," Shayla said, though she wasn't being completely honest. "But I am confused."

"I guess I figured I should just put it out there, let you know that I heard some of the rumors, but I don't believe them at all."

"As long as you're here for my mother and doing the best for her, that's what matters."

"Of course," Jennifer agreed. "We don't have to talk about this again."

"I'm going to go to my car, get my stuff," Shayla said, then walked past Jennifer and headed outside.

Why on earth had the nurse brought that up? Though she did understand that this was a small town and people talked, and maybe the nurse felt she was being supportive in some odd sort of way. Instead, her comments were intrusive, but Shayla was going to let it slide. She'd meant what she'd said. As long as the nurse was taking care of her mother, that's what mattered.

Shayla retrieved her suitcase and small travel bag from the car and returned to the house. She headed upstairs to her bedroom, pausing a moment before she opened the door. It had been so long…

She opened the door and peered inside. The room looked exactly as it had the day she'd left. The pink-and-blue comforter on the bed. The giant stuffed bear Lucas had given her propped up against the pillows. The photos on the walls of her in various dance outfits, either in the middle of a dance routine or posing with a trophy. Some photos of her and Hayley laughing and being silly.

It was almost eerie seeing everything as she'd left it. As if time had stood still in this room while the rest of the world had moved on.

Shayla stepped into the room with her belongings and closed the door. Her Sheridan Falls High letter jacket was still hanging on a hook behind the door, just where she'd left it. She had loved that jacket, but after the murders, she hadn't wanted any reminder of her high school days, so she'd left it behind when she'd taken off for Florida.

She stroked the red leather now, remembering all the sports she and Hayley had been involved in during high school. Dance, soccer, track, the swim team. They'd been overachievers when it came to sports, mostly because being involved in different activities kept them in shape for dance, their greatest love.

Shayla brought her bags to the foot of her bed. Again, she looked at the giant stuffed teddy bear. Lucas had given it to her the week before the murders, after they'd been dating for a month. Why she'd kept it, she didn't know. She'd just left it behind, along with other things she hadn't wanted to pack for her new life.

She went over to the teddy bear now and scooped it up. Then she tossed it into her closet where she wouldn't have to see it again.

Home, she thought as she returned to the bed and bounced on the soft mattress. It had taken nearly nine years, but she was finally home.

"I'm bored out of my mind here, Tavis," Griffin Woodward said. "All this girl wants to do is go from one high-end store to the next, buying makeup and dresses, and God knows what. Days like this, I could just shoot myself."

Tavis chuckled into the phone. "She's paying a pretty penny, remember that."

"I know," Griffin said, "which is why I haven't cocked my gun yet. I don't think there's any real threat to this girl. She probably just wants the prestige of having a bodyguard following her around."

"Which is fine by me," Tavis said. Sure, he enjoyed the adrenaline rush that came from a high-stakes case where there was tangible danger, but he preferred cases where there was no actual threat. Socialites who weren't in any real danger paid the bills just as much as celebrities who worried about stalkers.

Of course, with his line of work—personal security—there was no guarantee that any detail would be without danger. Even the rich, who wanted protection where there was no specific threat, could have angry people who wanted to hurt them. Enemies came in all forms, from jaded business partners to jealous peers, to bitter exes bent on doing harm. Tavis was prepared for all of that, and enjoyed performing the services of being a bodyguard for a myriad of people.

At least as the owner of his own company, he got to make all the rules. Unlike when he had worked for the Buffalo Police Department.

"Oh, got to go," Griffin said. "She's heading out of the store now."

"Update me if there's anything exciting," Tavis told him, a hint of humor in his voice.

"I doubt that, but yeah, I'll talk to you later."

Tavis was glad to hear that. He wanted an uneventful day.

As the sole proprietor of Forged in Steel Protection Services, he had two guys who worked for him. Griffin Woodward and Lenny Pinter. Lenny was currently out of town, providing protection services to a businessman at a convention. With a new and innovative product the man wanted to launch, he was worried about competitors who might pose a problem for him. But so far, there had been nothing eventful. Uneventful was always preferable.

Tavis's phone rang and he glanced at the screen. It was a number he didn't recognize with a prefix from Sheridan Falls. "Forged in Steel Protection Services."

"Tavis?"

"Yes, this is he."

"Hi, this is Deedee McKenzie. Shayla's cousin."

"Yes, of course. How are you?"

"I'm doing okay," she told him. "But I'm calling about Shayla."

Tavis rubbed the back of his neck. "Is she all right?"

"She just got back to town and I'm a bit worried about her. I've asked her to call you to see if she can secure your services. As you know, many people here don't like her, and I'm worried someone might want to hurt her."

Tavis rose from the chair where he was sitting in his home office. "What's going on?"

"She got a threat not too long ago. Someone who told her that if she returns to Sheridan Falls, she's going to be killed."

Tavis frowned, dragging a hand over his shortly cropped hair. He knew that after the murders years ago, Shayla had gotten several death threats. People in Sheridan Falls had been angry that two young people had been killed—understandably so—and with Lucas Carr on the lam, all of their anger had been directed at Shayla.

"Was it a phone call, email, something on social media?" Tavis asked.

"Email," Deedee answered.

Nine years later, and people were still threatening her. No wonder she'd left Sheridan Falls. Tavis himself felt a modicum of guilt over how he'd treated her in the wake of his cousin Hayley's death. He had firmly believed that Shayla had been hiding information about Lucas, despite her protests. It had just never made sense to him that she hadn't gone to the party that night. While he didn't think she'd asked Lucas to kill Hayley and Jonathan, he had been fairly certain that she'd known more about Lucas's whereabouts than she had admitted.

"You think the threat is credible?" Tavis asked.

"I've been telling her that I don't think the threats are real, but maybe that's just wishful thinking. She stopped by my restaurant for a bite to eat when she got back to town, and Tammy Hetrick was here. She had a few words with her and then threw a glass of water in her face. It hit me then that, despite the time that's passed, there are some people here who are still very, very angry with Shayla."

Tavis remembered that Tammy had been great friends with Hayley, but she'd also been friends with Shayla. Throwing water in her face, while not something that would physically hurt her, was still an attack.

"Have you asked her to call me? I happen to be available right now. I've got time. I can do the job."

"That's the problem," Deedee said. "I suggested that she hire you, but she's completely against the idea. She doesn't think she needs protection. You might remember, Shayla can be very stubborn."

"If she doesn't want to hire me, it's going to be pretty hard to protect her."

"I guess I just wanted to know if you're available, and I'm hoping I can convince her to call you in the next couple of days at least. Or…maybe you can drop by and see her? She's at her mom's place."

Should he drop by and pay her a visit? The idea gave him pause. He remembered the last time he had seen Shayla, and how their interaction had gone. She'd been devastated when he had pleaded with her to tell him where Lucas was. He could still remember the look in her eyes, the disbelief that he would even ask her that. He didn't know if stopping by to see her was a good idea.

"How's her mom doing?"

"Honestly, she's not really doing well. A few weeks ago, she was up and active. Then suddenly she got very weak. The doctors have told her that the chemo isn't working anymore. The cancer is eating her away."

"Man, I'm sorry to hear that."

"Thanks. She has nursing staff with her twenty-four-seven, but now that Shayla's back, she wants to be the one taking care of her mother most of the time. A nurse will still come by during the day, but Shayla intends to spend some quality alone time with her mom."

"That's understandable."

"Anyway," Deedee said, "I wanted to give you a heads-up, let you know what's going on, and hopefully my cousin will reach out to you."

"If she does, I'll be ready."

BY THE NEXT MORNING, Tavis hadn't heard from Shayla. Not that he had expected to, but Deedee's call had stayed with him throughout the night. The anniversary of the murders was coming up in just a couple of days, and because of that, tensions were probably high. The fact that someone was still threatening Shayla so many years later had him concerned. He was inclined to think the threat was real. Or, at least, should be taken seriously.

He decided to head over to her mom's place. He would take Shayla for coffee, and the two could talk. He hoped to penetrate her stubbornness and make her see reason.

Though Tavis had worked for the police department and founded his protection agency in the City of Buffalo, he still lived in Sheridan Falls. It wasn't a far trek to the city. Only thirty minutes outside downtown Buffalo without traffic, Sheridan Falls was a quieter area to live. Besides, Tavis had wanted to keep his roots in Sheridan Falls as he searched for clues to find Lucas.

It didn't take him long to get to Belmont Street. He drove slowly, and as his eyes wandered toward the Phillipses' house, they narrowed. Shayla was standing in the driveway, beside her vehicle. He could see her wide eyes even though he was around sixty feet away.

And then suddenly she turned and sprinted into the house, as if the devil himself were chasing her.

She hadn't seen him, had she? No, her gaze had been fixed on her windshield.

Tavis pulled to the curb and jumped out of his GMC Sierra. He surveyed his surroundings as he started up the driveway, searching for any visible threats. But it didn't take long for him to figure out what had spooked Shayla.

On the windshield of the car with Florida plates, he saw the words painted in white.

YOU WILL DIE.

Chapter Three

Shayla stood in the kitchen with her hands bracing the counter, her head reeling from the words painted on the windshield of her car.

YOU WILL DIE.

Who would have dared to put that there? And when?

The threat she had received just last week seemed far more real now. Not just someone trying to rattle her. Someone knew she was back in town, and they'd come to her mother's place to leave her a warning. This person clearly wasn't joking around.

Where was the nurse? Shayla had only started to head to her car because she'd wanted to pick up some cream, and Jennifer was running late. She hadn't even called to explain where she was. Shayla had sent her a text and gotten no reply.

The doorbell rang. It was probably Jennifer, and Shayla was irritated with her tardiness and lack of communication. She had a key. Why was she ringing the doorbell?

The doorbell rang again followed by a blurted "Shayla!"

That was a man's voice. A familiar voice…

"Shayla, open up. It's Tavis."

Tavis! Shock hit her like a punch to the gut. Why was he here?

But she quickly headed to the door, opened it, and as she stared into the face of her one-time crush, she felt an odd rush of sensation. Medium brown complexion, closely cropped hair. He looked the same, but different. The young man she'd once known had grown up. Eight and a half years ago, he had been tall and lanky. His once-thin frame had filled out with well-honed muscles. The once-boyish face now had a five-o'clock shadow, making him look a lot more mature. All of his new muscles were set in a six-foot-three-inch frame. The man was gorgeous.

Not that it mattered.

"Tavis," she said, hating how breathless she sounded. "What are you doing here?"

"Are you okay?" he asked. Then he looked over his shoulder at her car. "I saw you run into the house. When did that happen?"

Shayla exhaled sharply. "Come in."

She stepped backward, holding the door open, and Tavis entered the home. She led the way to the living room.

"Did you see anyone?" Tavis asked. "Hear anything?"

"No. I was heading to my car because I needed to run to the store to grab some cream for my coffee. The nurse is supposed to be here, I don't know where she is, so I was just going to run out for a moment while my mother is sleeping. And then I saw that written on my car. At first, I couldn't believe it. I thought my eyes were playing tricks on me. So I went closer... And saw that there really *was* a threat written on my windshield. It spooked me, so I turned around and ran back into the house."

Tavis cursed under his breath. "Deedee called me, told me that she thinks you could use a bodyguard."

"Oh, good grief. I'm sorry about that. I specifically told her that I didn't want a bodyguard."

"Actually, I'm glad she did. She was worried that calling me may be an overreaction on her part, but she figured why not be safe as opposed to sorry. Now you're in town for one day and you have a threat written on your car? Someone came to the house and put that on your car. I think you have to consider that this is a real threat, Shayla."

Shayla was momentarily taken aback by the way her name sounded on Tavis's lips. Maybe she was more rattled than she thought, because she wouldn't mind curling into his arms and having him hold her.

If he were the Tavis she'd known before the murders... But that Tavis had turned into someone else, someone angry and unforgiving where she was concerned.

"I guess it is," Shayla said. "But it's probably just someone else trying to scare me. I saw Tammy Taylor—Tammy Hetrick now—at Deedee's restaurant yesterday. She threw water in my face."

"Yeah," Tavis said. "Deedee told me."

"So I'm sure she got on the phone the moment she got home, or even before, and let everybody know that I was back. People know my mom is sick, and I'm sure they figured I would show up at some point. I just didn't expect that they would still hate me so much."

A moment of silence passed, then Tavis said, "I don't think everyone hates you. Obviously there are some people who have issues and haven't gotten over the murders—but that's because no one was ever brought to justice."

"How could anyone think that I would ever want to hurt Hayley?" she said in frustration, then clamped her lips shut. She didn't want to have this conversation with Tavis. Not now. Not after he had pretty much believed the worst about her as well nine years ago.

"How is your mother?" he asked softly.

"She's...not great," Shayla said, the words heavy in her throat. She didn't want to say what her heart didn't want to accept. "But I'm here now, and I'm going to help her get through this. I know I can."

The sound of the front door opening had both of them turning in that direction. Jennifer breezed into the house, offering an apology.

"Where were you?" Shayla asked, sounding harsh. But she hadn't expected someone who was being paid to take care of her mother to not even respond to her calls and texts.

"I'm so sorry. My phone died, and I had a flat tire. I'm sorry. It won't happen again."

Shayla's anger softened. "You didn't have a charger in the car for your phone?"

"It broke. And I stupidly forgot to charge my

phone last night." Jennifer held up a charger in a package. "I picked this up at the gas station once I got the spare tire put on. But I just raced here instead of calling as I was only a few minutes away."

Shayla wanted to be angry, but she found herself wondering why. Because of Jennifer's mess-up or because of anxiety? Lord knew that with the stress she was under, she wanted to lash out at someone.

"All right," Shayla said. "I'm glad you're here now and that you're safe."

"I'm really, really sorry," Jennifer reiterated. "Has your mother eaten yet?"

"No, she's been sleeping."

"Then I'll get to work on something for her to eat." She scooted past Tavis and Shayla, and went into the kitchen.

"I think you should call the police," Tavis said.

"Huh?" At first Shayla thought he was referring to the nurse, then caught on. "Oh, I don't think so."

"Why not?"

"Because…I don't want to make a bigger deal out of this than it is."

"A threat to your life is a big deal."

"Let me give it a couple of days. See if there's anything else." As Shayla looked at Tavis, she could see the disbelief in his eyes. He didn't understand why she wouldn't call the police. Shayla didn't know if it would make a difference calling the authorities. Would they be able to find out who'd actually done this? The person had probably been smart enough to wear gloves and not leave any prints. Besides, it was just one other thing for her to deal with now, and she had enough on her plate.

"So you haven't had coffee yet, based on the fact that you said you were heading out to get cream," Tavis said.

"No. Maybe that's why I'm extra cranky." She offered him a wry smile.

"Someone left a threat on your car. Of course you have a right to be cranky."

Shayla nodded as she folded her arms over her chest. He was right. But how concerned should she be? Was someone simply being a thorn in her side, trying to make her life miserable? She certainly hoped that was all it was.

"How about we go get a coffee together, talk for a bit? The nurse is here now. Is that okay?"

"I…I guess." Though sitting down and sharing coffee with Tavis wasn't exactly what she wanted to do. He probably felt a bit sorry for her, given what had happened, and she didn't want his pity.

"Honestly, you should be calling the police," he told her. "I know you don't want to, but this should be reported. Think about it. You can call later today, if you change your mind."

"Honestly, Tavis, it was probably just someone being an idiot." She was trying to convince Tavis of that fact as much as herself. "I'm used to this. Have been for nine years."

"You've still been getting threats all this time?" he asked.

"Not every day, but often enough. So, yeah, I'm used to it. If I called the police every time I got a threat, they'd probably bounce all my calls to voice-mail."

"This one was on your car," Tavis said. "It's different than an email threat. But it's your choice. Just think about it."

"One second," Shayla told him. Then she went to the kitchen, where she saw Jennifer peeling potatoes.

"Do you mind if I take off for a little bit? I'm gonna go get a coffee."

"Absolutely, go enjoy yourself. I'm here."

Shayla nodded. "Call me if there is any issue at all."

"I will."

Shayla was about to ask the nurse if she'd seen what had been scrawled on her car, but didn't bother. With Jennifer running late, she'd probably run right into the house and not even noticed.

"I'll see you later, then," Shayla told her. "Remember, call me if you need me."

"Take your time and enjoy your coffee," Jennifer said.

Shayla went back into the living room and smiled at Tavis. "All right. I'm ready to go."

No more than five minutes later, Tavis was pulling his vehicle into a spot in the center of town on Main Street, right in front of Molly's Café. He hopped out of the GMC Sierra, then went around and opened the passenger door for Shayla.

While he wasn't officially protecting her, he surveyed the area nonetheless before offering her a hand and helping her down from the vehicle. He saw Mr.

and Mrs. Chen sauntering hand in hand, which they said they'd been doing for the past fifty years since they'd gotten married. A woman on the other side of the street was walking a golden retriever. A couple of teenage girls dressed almost identically strolled by with their fancy frozen-coffee drinks.

No threats that he could see.

"Molly's Café," Shayla said as she stepped onto the sidewalk. "Molly Baxter?"

"The one and only."

"In high school she always said she wanted to open a café," Shayla said. "Good for her."

Tavis opened the door, and the door chimes sang. The coffee shop was fairly full, and again he looked around to make sure that he didn't see any specific sign of a threat.

Not that he knew what he was looking for.

Almost every head turned in their direction. And then mouths opened and eyes widened as people saw who was entering.

Shayla.

Tavis had expected this. Nine years ago, Shayla had been the topic of discussion for several months, even after she'd left town. People were now looking at her as though they were seeing a ghost.

He looked over his shoulder to where she stood rooted in the doorway. "Come on," he said. Moving to stand beside her, he placed a gentle hand on the small of her back. "People will get over this in a moment."

He walked into the café, and Molly, who was behind the counter, looked at him and gave him a smile.

Then her eyes wandered to Shayla and her entire face lit up.

"It seems at least one person doesn't hate me," Shayla muttered.

Tavis guided her to the line of customers, where two people were ahead of them: a man in a suit and a young woman scrolling through her social media feed. It took a few minutes to fill their orders before Tavis and Shayla stepped up to the counter.

"Hello, Tavis." Once again, Molly's eyes lit up as they landed on Shayla. "And is that really you, Shayla Phillips?"

"In the flesh," Shayla said, sounding pleasant.

"You've got to give me a hug, girl." Molly gestured for Shayla to lean across the counter. Tavis was shocked when he saw Molly heave her butt onto the polished black marble. But it was the only way to hug Shayla with the counter between them.

"It has been so long!" Molly said as she slid off the counter. "It's really good to see you again."

"It's really good to see you too," Shayla said. "I see you made your dream happen."

"Yep. Molly's Café." She sprayed down the counter and began wiping it. "I figure I drank so much coffee as a teen, I was destined to make a career out of it somehow." She chuckled. "My dad died the year after you left town. I used the money he left me to invest in this place."

"I love it," Shayla said.

"I was so sorry to hear about your mother," Molly said.

"Thank you. She's not doing that great, but I believe in keeping the faith until there's no more faith to be had."

"I agree with you. I'm praying for her. I'm sure all of the town is praying for her."

"Thank you. I do appreciate that."

Molly smiled again, her gaze volleying from Shayla to the lineup gathering behind her. "I'd better get your orders started. Tavis, I know you want a black coffee with two sugars."

"You know it. I keep it simple every day."

"Shayla, what can I get for you, hon?" Molly asked.

"I'd love a cappuccino. Caramel flavored," Shayla added, eyeing the menu on the back wall.

"One caramel cappuccino coming right up. You two go on and take a seat. I'll bring the coffees out to you."

Tavis paid then led Shayla through the coffee shop toward an available table near the back. The two-seater with plush chairs was by a window that faced State Street. He could feel the tenseness radiating from Shayla's body as she walked by each table, her gaze fixed forward despite the heads turning in her direction. And he couldn't blame her. The townsfolk in the coffee shop were blatantly staring as only people in small towns dared to do.

"I hate that everyone's looking at me like I don't belong here," Shayla said as she took a seat at the table.

Tavis took a seat across from her. "Ignore them. Like I said, people will get used to the fact that you're back before long. And life will go back to normal."

"Will it?" Shayla asked, a challenge in her voice. "It's been nine years and they haven't forgotten."

"You know how people are in this town. They will forget, trust me. They'll go back to their normal lives once they find something else worthy of talking about."

Shayla glanced down before meeting his gaze again. "I hope you're right."

"Molly was happy to see you. Not everyone here hates you."

"I guess not everyone." She opened her mouth as if she were about to say something else but then thought better of it.

"I know you're hesitant to hire me, but I want to let you know—"

"Tavis, why would you want to protect me?" Shayla said, interrupting him. "You don't even like me."

Her words hit him hard, at his core. He figured that was what she'd been about to say a moment earlier. It wasn't true, of course. He did like her. In fact, he'd always found her attractive, if a little young for him. Three years his junior had seemed like a world of difference back then. Now, of course, they were both adults...

Tavis quickly put a stop to that train of thinking, wondering why on earth that had even popped into his mind. Shayla was beautiful, with her bright brown eyes and long lashes, her thick head of curls and chocolate-colored skin. There was an effortless sexiness about her. Even with no makeup and dressed casually, her beauty radiated. Clearly, it had been too long since he'd been with a woman that just being in Shayla's company had the direction of his thoughts heading where he hadn't expected.

"You think I don't like you?" he asked. "That's not true, Shayla. I've always liked you."

Molly arrived then, her smile wide as she placed their orders on the table. "One black coffee with two sugars and one caramel cappuccino."

"Thank you," Shayla and Tavis said in unison.

The moment Molly was out of earshot, Tavis continued. "We haven't been in touch since you left town, but I was always your friend."

"And you were angry with me," Shayla said. "You think I forget our last conversation? You were livid. You believed I was protecting Lucas. That was the moment you stopped liking me, Tavis."

"That's not true." Tavis was silent for a moment. He sipped his coffee. "Hayley had just been killed, and I wasn't sure if you knew more than you were saying. I realize now that I was hard on you. But I was only trying to get answers."

"Everyone else in this town had turned on me and then you did too," Shayla said softly. She fiddled with her coffee cup before bringing it to her lips.

He stayed silent, letting her have a moment to enjoy the coffee. Though, given the faraway look in her eyes, he wasn't sure she was even tasting the beverage.

"I'm sorry that I was hard on you. But trust me, I always liked you. I was grieving my cousin's loss, trying to get answers."

"I was grieving too. I needed…" Her voice trailed

off. "It doesn't matter what I needed. It was a long time ago."

"Hey," Tavis said softly. He reached across the table and put his hand on hers, surprising himself. "You were hurt. It does matter."

"I'm fine," Shayla insisted.

"I'm here for you now," Tavis told her. "And I'm not about to let anyone hurt you. You're an old friend. I'm happy to provide protection services free of charge."

"Oh, absolutely not." Shayla moved her hand away. "I don't want charity."

"It wouldn't be charity. Call it me making up for the past. For me being hard on you when I should have known that you would never protect Lucas."

"Whatever you want to call it, I don't need to be protected. And I wouldn't want you to pass up other work to babysit me."

Tavis sipped more of his coffee, and decided not to push the issue of protection for the time being, but he had something else he wanted to discuss with her. "I know you might not want me to ask you this, considering our last conversation years ago. Especially given what you just said. But did you ever hear from Lucas any time over the past nine years?"

Shayla's eyes widened, registering her disappointment. "I can't believe you would ask me that. You just said that you believed I wouldn't keep Lucas's whereabouts secret—"

"That doesn't mean he didn't call you, or send you a message—even if he never told you where he was. I'm just wondering if you ever heard a word from him in some shape or form."

"I didn't. I've never heard from him. Not once. And I don't know what happened to him after the night of the party. He left town and dropped me, just like he dropped everyone else."

Tavis thought about her words. It was beyond frustrating that Lucas had disappeared without a trace. Tavis had used his resources at the police department to search for him and had never come up with a shred of evidence indicating where he might be. It wasn't impossible that he was living off the grid, or had stolen someone's ID and assumed a new identity. He'd probably hightailed it clear across the country to California, or Washington. Maybe he'd even crossed the border into Canada. All Tavis knew was that he wouldn't rest until he had his cousin's killer apprehended and paying for his crimes.

"Hey," he said softly as Shayla was sipping her coffee and gazing outside. There was tension between them, and he needed to clear things up. "Please know that I never hated you. I was disappointed and upset, and I judged you wrongly."

Shayla said nothing.

"I didn't ask you about Lucas right now because I believed you were keeping anything from me, but we haven't seen each other in almost nine years, and it's possible you could have heard from him during that time. This is the first time we're talking about it. I had to ask."

"And now you know."

Tavis nodded. "Yes, now I know." He paused. "Years ago, I never believed that you would ever *want* to protect Lucas. What I did think was that you were probably scared of him, maybe had even been threatened by him into staying silent. It crossed my mind that if you'd lied originally, you wouldn't ever think you could come clean with the truth, scared that people would be even more angry with you if you admitted that you knew where he'd gone."

When Shayla opened her mouth to protest, Tavis continued. "Hear me out. I said that's what crossed my mind back then. And that's why I pressed you hard for answers. But I can see now—I know now— that you wouldn't lie about that. You loved Hayley like a sister. And you would want her killer brought to justice just as much as I would."

"I did love her like a sister," Shayla said, her voice hitching. Then she straightened her spine. She glanced left for the first time, into the café at large, then gasped softly. "Oh my God, that's Jonathan's grandfather. And the way he's looking at me…"

Tavis quickly looked in that direction. And sure enough, Donny Bozzo was staring at Shayla, his gaze unyielding and serious.

"Ignore him," Tavis said. "That's the best way to handle anyone who gives you a hard time. Do your best to ignore any negativity."

Shayla sipped more of her cappuccino. Her chest rose and fell with a heavy breath. She glanced in Donny's direction once more, this time offering the man a small smile before returning her attention to Tavis.

"You know," she began, "I came back to Sheridan Falls thinking that I needed to hide out and be remorseful and afraid of what people would think. I almost didn't want to say yes to coffee with you because I didn't want to face anyone in the town. But the truth is I have no reason to be guilty about anything. I have no reason to hide my face. I did nothing wrong. And I'm not about to act as though I did."

"Good."

"I just wish it was as easy to not care," she went on. "But I'll get there."

Shayla's eyes wandered toward Jonathan's grandfather again, and Tavis followed her line of sight. The older man was now leaving the coffee shop. Because of her? Well, let him go. At least he hadn't decided to come over to their table and harass Shayla.

"We should probably go now," Shayla said. "I can pop into the variety store next door and get some cream, then we can head back to my house."

Before Tavis had a chance to respond, Shayla shot to her feet. She reached into her own wallet and put the tip on the table.

Tavis rose to join her. "Thanks for agreeing to have coffee with me. Hopefully it won't be a one-time thing."

Shayla tucked a strand of her curly black hair behind her ear, not meeting his eyes. "Maybe."

Sheesh, why had he even suggested getting together for coffee again? He'd made it sound like an invitation for a date.

"If you want," he said. "You know…to talk."

"Sure," Shayla said softly. "I'll let you know."

Unlike when they'd arrived, she took the lead, heading to the coffee shop's exit, waving at Molly as she passed. Tavis followed her, matching her quick strides.

She opened the door and stepped onto the sidewalk, and then Tavis saw her body seize with fear. A quick glance to the right told him why.

Donny Bozzo stood on the sidewalk with a gun aimed at Shayla.

"Don't you move!" he cried. "Because of you, my grandson is dead. And now you're finally going to pay for your crimes."

Chapter Four

In a flash, Tavis was in front of Shayla, protecting her with his body. "Whoa, Donny. Put the gun down."

"No," Donny said, his resolve steely even though his voice quivered. "It's time she pay for what she did. She had my grandson killed."

"That's not true," Shayla said, but Tavis quickly put up a hand to silence her.

Tavis looked at the old man, assessing the situation. Was he crazy enough to pull the trigger? It wasn't something that Tavis could risk, and he slipped his hand beneath his jacket, placing it on the handle of his gun. As a bodyguard, he had a license to carry. And having been a police officer, he knew very well how to use the SIG Sauer.

But he didn't want to pull his own gun out and make an already-tense situation even worse. However, he wanted to be ready in case Donny decided to do something stupid.

"Donny, lower your gun," Tavis repeated.

"I'm not gonna kill her, which is more than she did for my grandson. But I called the police. They're on their way. They're going to arrest her."

As if on cue, the sirens sounded and seconds later two cop cars whizzed around the corner, coming to a screeching stop in front of the coffee shop. Sheriff Thompson jumped out of the first vehicle, and one of his deputies, Deputy Campbell, jumped out of the second vehicle, both rushing forward, their hands on their guns.

The sheriff's eyes volleyed between Tavis and Donny. "Whoa, whoa, whoa," he said, sounding surprised. "Donny, what are you doing?"

"There she is," Donny said, pointing the gun in Shayla's direction. "The one who had my grandson killed. Arrest her."

"Donny, lower the gun," Sheriff Thompson said. "We don't want anyone getting hurt today."

"Sheriff, you need to take her in," Donny stressed.

The sheriff approached Donny slowly. "You know I'm gonna do my job. If she is responsible, she will pay. Trust me on that."

"Of course she's responsible!" Donny yelled.

Behind Tavis, Shayla clung to his back. He felt a weird sense of satisfaction that she was trusting him, given the undoubted tension between them. Not that she had much choice, but still it felt good that he was here for her.

So much for idle threats.

The sheriff drew his own weapon, but kept it lowered. "Now, Donny, don't make me tell you again. I don't want to have to arrest you. Leave this matter to the law." He gave him a stern look. "Lower your gun."

"As long as you're going to make sure she doesn't

get away with what she did. She's a killer, even if she didn't pull the trigger herself!"

"I will take care of this matter," Sheriff Thompson said.

Finally, Donny lowered his gun, his shoulders slumping, as though all of his energy had oozed out of his body. He began to weep softly.

Tavis knew how intense the grief was. He'd lost his cousin. But this wasn't the way to handle the situation.

Pulling himself together, Donny looked at Tavis with contempt. "And what are you doing with her anyway? She killed your cousin!"

"As the sheriff said, the law will deal with Shayla as necessary," Tavis said. Behind him, Shayla flinched.

Deputy Campbell moved forward, taking the gun from Donny's hand and then guiding him to his pickup truck. Tavis couldn't help thinking that if this were anyone else, the sheriff and deputy would have taken him down on the ground in a flash. Waving a gun around in the center of town was dangerous. Uncalled for. A clear threat. But they were treating old man Donny with kid gloves.

"You're not going to arrest him?" Shayla asked. "He pulled a gun on me. He could have killed me!"

"Ah, Donny is no harm," the sheriff said, and twirled the edge of his gray, handlebar mustache. "Besides, he's all tore up over his grandson. Can't say I blame him. But Donny…he's all talk, no bite. He called the police, told us that a crime was in progress. That's how he got us here." The sheriff threw a warning glance at Donny over his shoulder. "That wasn't right, Donny. You shouldn't have made a false claim of a crime in progress."

"As far as I'm concerned, a crime is in progress right now. A felon escaping the law as she did nine years ago."

Shayla pressed her face against Tavis's back, and he wasn't sure if she was crying. He turned and gathered her in his arms, and felt her melt against him. He stroked his hand over her hair, not caring that he was maybe getting too close. He just wanted her to feel okay. To feel safe.

"That's enough now," Deputy Campbell said to Donny. "Put the gun back in the glove compartment. That's it." He closed the door once Donny was sitting upright in the driver's seat. "You have a good day now, Donny. Say hello to Emma for me."

"Unbelievable," Shayla muttered. "They just treated him like a two-year-old who dropped an ice-cream cone."

As Donny drove off, the sheriff approached Tavis. "Why am I not surprised to see you mixed up in this?" he asked.

"Mixed up in what?" Tavis asked. "I was here getting coffee with Shayla, we came out and Donny had a gun pulled."

"Always chasing trouble," the sheriff mused. He stepped toward Shayla. "You all right?"

Shayla nodded. "Yes," she said, but her voice was feeble.

"So you're back in town."

"Yes. My mother… She's sick."

"Yeah, I heard. I'm real sorry about that. You convey that to her for me, will you? Let her know that I'm wishing her well."

"Of course," Shayla told him. She paused and said, "So you're not going to arrest Donny? He gets to pull a gun on me without any consequences?"

"Donny took his grandson's death real hard. Now, I know you said you never had anything to do with it, and I believe you. But a lot of people in this town felt you were hiding some vital information. Maybe you were afraid to tell us what you knew?" The sheriff's voice ended on a question.

"No," Shayla said. "I held back nothing."

Sheriff Thompson nodded. "And since you've been gone all these years, have you ever been in touch with Lucas? Do you know where he is now?"

"I have no clue where he is. I never heard from him after the day of the murders. Please," Shayla said, sounding exasperated, "you have to believe me."

The sheriff nodded, seeming to believe her. "All right. But if you hear anything at all, let me know. No one's ever paid for this crime, and it would mean a lot in this town if we could see the killer brought to justice."

"I'm sure it would. I just wish people would stop blaming me," Shayla added with the hint of bitterness.

"Tell him about the threat on your car," Tavis said.

The sheriff's eyes widened. "Threat?"

Shayla hesitated for a moment then spoke. "I don't know if it's really anything. But someone wrote a threat on my car. It read 'you will die.'" Shayla shrugged. "I don't know."

She was downplaying this, but with Donny pulling a gun on her, the threat on her car and even Tammy accosting her in the restaurant, it was clear to Tavis that she still had quite a few enemies in this town. "She's had some email threats as well," Tavis said. "I'm a bit worried that someone might really want to hurt her. So you keep your ear to the ground, sheriff? If you hear anything, make sure you take it seriously."

Sheriff Thompson's lips curled, but there was no cheer behind the smile. "Of course," he said, his tone clipped. "I've been doing this job for a long time, Tavis. I've always got my ear to the ground."

"That's all I ask."

"I hope that means you plan to leave this matter to law enforcement. I can handle the people in this town."

His gaze lingered on Tavis, a silent warning. There was no love lost between the two men. Then he turned and headed back to his cruiser.

SHAYLA SAT CURLED in the passenger seat as Tavis drove her back to her mother's place. The events that had transpired had her shaken. She knew people hated her and didn't want her back in Sheridan Falls. But it was worse than that. Maybe they wouldn't be happy until she was stoned in the town square.

That was likely an exaggeration, but with Donny pulling a gun on her, could she be blamed for her macabre thoughts? The incident had her rethinking her return to her hometown.

She'd had no choice. She had to be here for her mother, no matter the risk.

"Hey," Tavis said softly, interrupting her thoughts. "You okay? Obviously, you can't be fully okay. But how are you doing?"

"I'm wishing I never had to come back to this town," Shayla said honestly. There was nothing here for her, except for her mother. And, of course, her cousin and aunt and uncle, but this was too hard. More than she'd bargained for.

"If it's any consolation, I don't think Donny was going to hurt you. He saw you, was shocked, and obviously overreacted."

"And then got the royal treatment from the sheriff's department." Shayla made a face. "They need to at least take things like this seriously."

"I agree with you. Donny deserved more than a talking-to."

"They barely did even that." Shayla sighed. "What's the point of me calling them about any threat or telling them what happened to my car? I don't think they're going to handle it the way law enforcement should."

"That's where I come in," Tavis said. He glanced at her, and she met his gaze, but she didn't say anything.

"I'm good at what I do," Tavis went on. "For example, I verified the nurse's story with one look at her car."

"What do you mean?"

"She said she'd had a flat tire. When we left for coffee, I saw that, indeed, she did have the donut tire on her car."

Shayla made a face. "Do you suspect her of something?"

"It's my job to check out everything. Everyone."

"But surely the nurse… She was caring for my mother before I even came to town."

"Like I said, it's my job to check out everything and everyone. And at least her story checked out. She's got the donut on her car, so yes, she was late because she had a flat tire. When you don't know where a threat is coming from, you can't dismiss any possible angles."

Shayla supposed he was right. He was the professional, after all.

"I think it's wise to have me watching your back," he continued. "I won't be intrusive. I can shadow you, watch your house, make sure there are no signs of danger. But given the temperature of things around here—and the fact that the anniversary of the deaths is in a couple of days—it's probably best for me to stick around and make sure you're okay until all of this blows over."

Shayla said nothing, because how could she argue his point? Had she been at the coffee shop on her own, what would have happened? Would Donny have gone too far? Would he have been too angry to listen to reason and pulled the trigger?

She shuddered at the idea.

Tavis turned onto Belmont Street and moments later was pulling up in front of her house.

"Thank you," she said, facing him. "For the coffee, for everything."

"You didn't say whether or not you agree to have me provide you protection services."

Shayla offered him a small smile. "Do I have a choice? I don't think you're going to take no for an answer."

"You're right," Tavis said.

Shayla shrugged. She was stuck with Tavis, whether she wanted to be or not. "By the way, it seems like you and the sheriff aren't the best of friends."

"You figured that out?"

"I could feel the tension between the two of you. He was polite as he spoke, but it was clear that he was telling you to back off. And then he made that comment about you always being around when there's trouble."

"Yeah, I'm definitely not one of Thompson's favorite people."

Shayla looked at him, waiting for him to continue. When he didn't, she asked, "Why? What's the story between you two?"

"He and I don't exactly see eye to eye."

Shayla waited. Was that all he was going to give her?

"Remember, I used to be a cop. The whole reason I became a cop was to try to find Lucas and bring him to justice. I didn't apply to the sheriff's department here. I figured I wanted to be in a bigger city where I could ideally have more resources. So I went to Buffalo, applied. Got through there. I also thought maybe Lucas was back in Buffalo, because that's where he'd grown up. I figured it might be easier to find him there, because he clearly wasn't in Sheridan

Falls. Anyway, let's just say I did a lot of digging on people in the town and broke a few rules trying to find answers as to what happened to Hayley. Sheriff Thompson always felt I was pushing too far, going around his authority to get answers."

"And were you?"

Tavis shrugged. "I didn't want to leave any stone unturned. The way it seemed to me, Sheriff Thompson had given up. As far as he was concerned, Lucas had taken off and wouldn't be found, so why waste resources searching for him? That wasn't okay with me. And I couldn't understand why it was okay with him."

"So you're a bit of a rebel," Shayla surmised.

"Determined," Tavis countered. "Determined to get justice for Hayley." His gaze wandered off. He was silent for several moments. "But I failed to do that."

As much as Shayla had been the brunt of his wrath and anger years before, she felt for him now. She'd lost her best friend. And because of the way she had been treated, she hadn't fully considered other people's grief. Tavis had lost his cousin. It must have been excruciating for him.

"I'm not sure if I ever said that I'm sorry that you lost Hayley…" Shayla began. "I know, I lost her too. But what I mean is I was so focused on my own grief, my own pain, defending my name, I'm not sure I really considered how hurt you were. As family to her."

"I know you cared. She was your best friend. You loved her same as I did."

"Absolutely," Shayla said. "I still can't believe

what happened. All these years later, in some ways it feels like a dream. A nightmare."

"And you have no idea why Lucas would do this?"

Shayla threw her hands up and slapped them down on her thighs. "All I can think is that they were drinking, he was stupid, he had a gun. I don't know… But something went down. Maybe it was a fight with Jonathan, and Hayley was just there. Maybe Hayley took out her anger with me on him. A million things have crossed my mind, but at the end of the day, I don't have any answers because I wasn't there."

"I know."

"Do you? Do you really believe me?"

"I told you earlier, I do believe you."

Shayla's gaze wandered out the window. Then her eyes narrowed. Was she seeing what she thought she was seeing? There was a scratch along the entire right side of her car!

"Oh my God."

"What?" Tavis asked, instantly sitting straight and sounding on edge.

"There's a scratch along the side of my car. Maybe it was there before and I didn't notice. Or did someone else come and do this while we were gone?"

Tavis opened his door, then got out. Shayla did the same, heading straight toward her car. She cursed under her breath when she saw how deep the scratch was.

"I didn't notice that before," Tavis said.

"But did you see all of my car?" she asked.

"I didn't specifically look, no. I was checking out the nurse's vehicle."

Despite the warmth of the day, a chill ran down Shayla's spine. She wrapped her arms around her body. "Did someone come here while we were out? My mother is in the house. She's sick. She doesn't need the stress. And neither do I. I can't handle this…"

Tavis put his hands on her shoulders, and she didn't move away from him. She accepted the comfort he was offering her, trying not to think about how good it felt being so close to him.

"There are a couple of repair shops in town," Tavis began, "you want me to take your car somewhere?"

"No," she said. She didn't want to lean on him for everything. She was independent, and she would deal with this. "I'll take care of it later. Or maybe I should just let it sit. No point fixing it just for someone else to come along and vandalize it again."

"No one is going to be able to vandalize your car while I'm around."

Shayla turned, stepping away from Tavis's touch. Looking up at him, she asked, "Starting now?"

"Actually, if you don't mind, there are a couple things I need to do. Since I wasn't prepared to start this job immediately, I've got to check in with a couple of my guys at the office, catch up on a little bit of paperwork. I'll go home, grab my laptop. Then I can stay in the car and do what I need to do."

"That's perfectly fine," Shayla said. "Especially considering I didn't expect that you would even be doing this job for me. I…I can't pay you—*yet*. With my mother's health care—"

"I already offered to do this pro bono. You're a

friend. I'm not going to stand by and let something happen to you. So don't worry about that."

"Okay," Shayla said softly. She knew not to push the issue. But when she could, she would pay him something. "When do you think you'll be back?"

"Give me an hour. Hour and a half tops."

ONCE TAVIS LEFT, Shayla figured she may as well find a local body shop where she could take her car. Though she had contemplated leaving it and letting anyone else in the town have a go at it, she realized she couldn't do that. The idea of looking out every day or even driving the car with that threat on the windshield was something she wouldn't do. So she looked in the phone book and found two body shops. She chose to go to the closest one. Lucky's Auto Shop.

When she arrived and went inside, she saw a familiar face behind the counter. Older, but definitely familiar.

"Chase?" she asked.

"Shayla!" the man boomed. He was her age, twenty-seven, but he looked at least ten years older. He had changed quite significantly since he'd dated Shayla's cousin, Deedee, back in high school. Then, Chase had been a football player, with a full head of thick hair and a muscular body. These days, his once-shaggy blond locks had prematurely thinned on top, he'd put on considerable weight, which hid any muscles, and he had a sizable beer belly.

"I heard you were back in town," he said, sounding pleased.

"Yeah. My mom— You probably heard…"

"I did. Cancer sucks, man."

"That it does."

"What brings you into my shop?"

"This is yours?" Shayla asked.

"Yep. You might remember that I liked to work on cars. They say make your passion your job and it never feels like work, right? So, I decided to open up an auto body shop here in town. We do oil changes, mechanics work and also bodywork. It's been good."

"Then I guess I'm in the right spot. Someone keyed my car. It needs to be repainted."

"Damn," Chase said. "Sorry to hear that."

"And so you're not shocked, something's written on the windshield of my car too. I tried scraping it, but I couldn't get it all off. Someone wrote a threat telling me that I'm going to die." She spoke casually, as if the threat was no big deal. But she couldn't stop wondering if someone truly wanted her dead.

Chase's eyes registered shock. "That happened here?"

"You know people here have long memories. Anyway, can you come out and take a look at it, then give me a quote for how much it will cost and how long it will take?"

"Sure thing."

As Chase headed out from behind the counter and walked ahead of Shayla to the door, she mused at how differently two people could change over the years. While Chase looked visibly older, and more out of shape compared to his fitter younger self, Tavis had grown into an even more attractive and strong man who must have women's heads turning constantly.

But why was she even thinking of Tavis?

Because he was gorgeous and strong and he'd protected her from possibly getting shot. Despite how he'd hurt her, he had been her crush, and seeing a more mature and sexier version of him still stoked a reaction from her.

"I hear you married Lisa Middleton," Shayla said.

"Yep. Eight years now. I guess Deedee told you."

"She did." Along with her commentary about how much she despised Lisa, who had made a play for Chase while Deedee had been dating him.

"Me and Lisa have three little ones now. Two boys and a girl."

"Ah, so sweet," Shayla said. Though years had passed since Deedee and Chase's bitter breakup, they didn't talk. Deedee seemed to have never gotten over the way their relationship had ended. The fact that he was currently married to Lisa was probably the biggest reason why she wouldn't talk to him.

"I think your cousin still hates me," Chase said as he opened the door, smiling wryly. "Which is just as well, I guess. Because Lisa doesn't want me talking to her. I think she still sees Deedee as a rival, even though I married her. And you know what they say, happy wife, happy life."

"Right." Shayla headed to her vehicle, which was parked in the shop's lot. "That's my car." She walked along the right side and pointed to the scratch. "You can see where it was keyed."

Chase bent onto his haunches and smoothed a finger over the scratch. "They keyed you good."

Shayla rounded the front of her vehicle. "And this

is the windshield. It's some sort of glossy paint, I think. Hopefully it won't be any trouble for you to get it off."

Chase joined Shayla at the front of her car. "You weren't kidding. That's a definite threat."

"You can clean it up?"

"The windshield's no problem," Chase told her. "But that scratch...it's along the entire length of your car. That means all those panels need to be repainted. If it was just the door, I could do that section alone. But I'll have to match everything, and that means doing almost a full paint job for you."

Shayla winced. Once again, she wondered if she should leave this to be done now, or wait until the townsfolk had fully taken out their wrath on her. What if there was more damage afterward?

But she had already spoken with her insurance company, and she was going to go ahead and do this. She'd filed an official report with the sheriff's department before bringing her car here.

At least with the car in the shop, it wouldn't be in the driveway for a couple of days.

"I can take care of this for you," Chase said. "I'll need two days. Maybe three."

"That's fine with me."

"Let's head back in and I'll get the work order started for you," he said.

The two wandered back into the shop and Chase went behind the counter and got onto the computer. He asked her for further information. She gave it.

"So, you ever hear from Lucas?" Chase asked.

"No, never heard from him. I don't know what

happened to him, and I don't know why he did what he did."

Chase harrumphed. "I used to think that Lucas was a nice guy. I mean, he wasn't perfect—just like me and my brother weren't—we did some crazy stuff. But I didn't expect him to murder anybody."

"So maybe three days to fix my car?" Shayla asked. She didn't want to talk about Lucas anymore.

"With the amount of painting on all those panels, yeah, I'd give it three days."

"Okay. I can survive three days." Her mother had a car, if necessary. She could use that. People would probably be less likely to vandalize her mother's car. At least her mother hadn't had to bear the brunt of the wrath for her daughter's perceived sins.

"If you don't mind me saying, I never understood what attracted you to Lucas. You two seemed so different."

"He was new to town, he asked me out," Shayla said by way of explanation.

"Yeah, but he was such a rebel. You didn't care that he sold weed?"

"I really didn't know much of what he was up to."

"Come on," Chase said, then leaned forward and said in a lowered voice, "You had to know some of the stuff he was involved in."

"I heard a lot of rumors after he took off, but before that, I was involved with my dance and sports. And he probably didn't want to tell me about his bad habits. Besides, Lucas and I really weren't together that long. We'd barely been dating when…when…"

Her voice trailed off. There was no need to finish her statement.

"Yeah, but you had to have known *some* stuff. Like he probably told you who he sold drugs to, that sort of thing?"

This was the first time anyone had asked her such a question, and Shayla felt as though she were in the twilight zone. "No. I know nothing about any of that. Why are you asking?"

"I just heard some stuff, is all. Wondered if you knew much about it."

"More than the allegation that he sold weed?"

Chase shrugged. "I heard he used to flash a gun around sometimes."

"You and Alex hung out with him a lot. Did you ever see him with a gun?"

Chase's eyes narrowed, as though surprised that she'd turned the line of questioning on him.

"You'd probably know a lot more of what he was up to than I did," Shayla added.

Slowly, Chase shook his head. "My dad's the sheriff, remember? He wasn't stupid enough to flaunt a gun in our faces."

"I suppose not."

An easygoing smile came on his face. "I guess I've lived in this town too long. We're always nosy. Don't mind our business."

Shayla smiled tightly.

"But I always got the sense that he was connected to something bigger. You know, he'd come from Buffalo, said his parents wanted him to have a change of scenery and get away from his bad friends. I thought

he was still connected to the big city. I don't know...
I just feel like he was involved in some kind of bigger
criminal enterprise. Maybe he was running weapons, that kind of thing."

"Running weapons? That's a bit of a stretch, isn't
it?" None of this sounded familiar to Shayla, and the
little she knew of Lucas, she didn't believe that he
was part of some big criminal enterprise. Leave it to
small-town folks to have big imaginations. She knew
he had a bad-boy reputation, but she'd always thought
he was fronting. Acting tough so no one bothered
him. But she hadn't really known him all too well.

"Did you ever talk to your dad?" Shayla asked.
"Tell him your theories? Are you thinking he had
help killing Hayley and Jonathan?"

"Not sure. Just thinking off the top of my head,
I guess. Wondering if you knew anything specific
about what he was up to."

"I knew nothing."

Chase went back to typing in whatever information on the computer, then he printed out some paperwork for her to sign. "If you sign here, that authorizes
me to do the work. That's the price, but I'll be send-
ing it off to your insurance company. If there are
any complications, I can call you and let you know,
but I don't expect there to be. This is pretty routine."

"Sounds great." Shayla scrawled her signature on
the form. "Thanks so much. I look forward to hearing from you."

"Hey," Chase began, "you need a ride home?"

Shayla hadn't fully thought of that. She considered

calling her cousin, or taking a long walk. "Actually, I was going to call my cousin."

"Deedee," Chase said. "How's she doing?"

"She's good. She bought a restaurant. Perhaps you've been there?"

"Haven't been there yet. Lisa has forbid me to ever go there." He chuckled. "Anyway, I don't mind giving you a ride home if you need one. I've got a couple of guys working on cars. They can cover the front for me."

Shayla's cell phone rang. She saw Deedee's face flashing on her screen. "Speak of the devil," she said to Chase. Then she quickly answered the call. "Hey, I was just about to call you."

"Where are you?" Deedee asked, sounding somewhat harried.

"I'm at Lucky's Auto Shop."

"You are?"

"Yeah, I was just gonna call you for a ride home." She glanced toward Chase, gave him a wave and exited the store so she could speak to Deedee outside without worrying that anyone was overhearing the conversation. The warm summer air enveloped her. "Why do you sound so worried? Did you talk to Tavis?"

"Tavis?"

"Deedee, I know you. What's going on?"

"It's your mother."

Shayla's stomach spasmed. "My mother. Is she okay?"

"I'm coming to get you right away."

Chapter Five

Shayla barely breathed as she waited for Deedee to pull up in front of Lucky's. And when she did, she could see the stress on her cousin's face.

"Is she okay?" Shayla asked without preamble as she hopped into the car.

"She started having trouble breathing," Deedee told her. "I was with her at the time and...I'm not gonna lie, it was very frightening."

"Oh God," Shayla whimpered.

"I rushed to get you because I know you would want to be there, but I just spoke to the nurse and she's calmed down now. So don't be too upset. But your mother was asking for you, and she was very irritated."

"Because she thinks this is the end?" Shayla couldn't help asking. Though she wanted to be positive, wanted to believe that her mother was going to pull through, the ugly alternative couldn't escape her mind.

"I'm not sure. All I know is that I was really worried, but thank God the nurse updated me. She said your mother's breathing is regulated."

"Why didn't Jennifer call me?"

"Because I was at the house when it happened, and I told her that I'd track you down."

"And no one called 9-1-1?"

"You know your mother's wishes," Deedee said softly, and she and Shayla exchanged glances.

Yes, Shayla knew that her mother didn't want any lifesaving measures. She just didn't agree with the decision.

"What's going on with you?" Deedee asked. "You asked if I'd spoken to Tavis, and you were at Lucky's. Why?"

Shayla quickly filled her in on what had happened with the threat on the car as well as the vandalism. "So I figured I'd bring the car to a body shop, and it turns out that Chase works there."

"He owns the shop," Deedee clarified. "If you'd told me about this ahead of time, I would have told you to go to the other body shop."

There was no love lost between her cousin and Chase, though they'd dated years ago. Shayla remembered Deedee being angry at Chase after the breakup. She'd said he left her for Lisa because Chase was white and Deedee was Black. At least, that was what Deedee believed, though Shayla hadn't been so sure. The one thing that Shayla had liked about this place was that people didn't seem to be hung up on color. Though the town was small, the population was diverse. They looked at each other for who they were, not the color of their skin.

"Something else happened," Shayla said, and exhaled a sigh that signified the magnitude of the situation. "I ran into Jonathan's grandfather. He pulled a gun on me."

"What?" Deedee exclaimed.

"I was with Tavis. He jumped into action to protect me. But I don't think that Donny was going to shoot me. He just wanted to make sure I didn't go anywhere. At least, that's what he said. He'd called the cops to arrest me."

As they neared Belmont Street, Deedee said, "So, have you decided to hire Tavis then? I think it's a good idea. Especially with everything you just told me."

"After what happened with Donny, I don't think if I told him no, he would listen. So, why not? Better safe than sorry."

"Good. Someone needs to be looking out for you."

Deedee pulled up in front of the house, and Tavis's Sierra was already there. Shayla jumped out and started to rush up the driveway. Tavis exited his pickup and called out to her, but Shayla said, "Deedee will fill you in. My mom needs me."

SEEING HER MOTHER awake and calm had waves of relief washing over Shayla. It had been one thing to hear Deedee say that her mother had recovered from whatever breathing spell had alarmed them all, but another to see her looking okay. Still, Shayla was frazzled nonetheless. She hoped there wasn't another incident like this that had her fearing she might be losing her mother. Thankfully, as her mother's pain had increased and her anxiety grew, the nurse had been there to administer the appropriate medicine to calm her down. Maybe her mother had just needed her to be by her side, because seeing Shayla now seemed to perk her up.

Shayla felt guilty for leaving, but she had needed to take care of her vehicle. And she could never have predicted that at the moment she'd left, her mother would experience a mini crisis. When she'd gone to Lucky's Auto Shop, her mother had been sleeping peacefully.

"I'm sorry I wasn't here for you, Mom," Shayla said softly.

"I'm okay now, baby. For some reason, I woke up and was afraid. I don't fully remember, but I had some sort of bad dream. About you. That you were in danger. And when I woke up and you weren't here…I was so scared."

Shayla hated to hear that she was the cause for her mother's distress. "You don't need to worry about me, Mom."

Her mother chuckled softly, but there was pain behind the sound. "Oh, you'll understand one day when you have a child. There's no such thing as not worrying about them."

"So I've heard."

"Are you all right?" her mother asked. "I know you never wanted to come back here, and I know people haven't been kind to you. I'm just hoping that when they see you out and about now, they'll be nicer."

Shayla couldn't tell her mother what had happened with Donny, or with Tammy, or even her car. There was no way she would add more stress to what her mother was already experiencing. So she didn't.

"I haven't really run into many people, but either people are keeping their opinions to themselves or they've put it behind them," she said. Her mother gave her a doubtful look, but Shayla squeezed her hand. "Please, Mom, I'm fine."

"Okay, darling. But be careful. I don't know why I had that dream, but it left me with a bad feeling. I just want you to be safe."

"What about you, Mom? How has everyone been toward you?" Shayla hoped that they hadn't been horrible to her, that her mother hadn't stayed here despite bad treatment.

"After the initial shock of the murders and people feeling you might've had something to do with it, they really didn't see me as a bad guy. I know they lashed out at you, but there was a bit of sympathy for me after you left town. People feeling bad that you were my only child and now you'd gone, and you were caught up in this mess. Surprisingly, they didn't come after me the way I thought they might."

"I'm glad for that," Shayla said. Her mother had told her as much over the years, yet she wasn't certain she'd told her the truth. But maybe that did explain why her mother hadn't been keen on leaving and heading down to Miami. She'd been more or less treated well in the town, so she hadn't had a reason to escape.

Unlike Shayla.

"Here's one more reason for your mind to be at ease," Shayla began. "You'll be happy to know that I've taken a precaution to make sure that I am definitely safe. You remember Tavis?"

"Oh yes, of course I remember Tavis Saunders.

You used to have a crush on him," her mother said, a smile touching her lips.

"That's ancient history. But he has a protection service agency, and Deedee put him in touch with me. He's decided to offer me protection services— out of an abundance of caution—to make sure I'm safe while I'm in town."

"You agreed to that?" her mother asked.

"You know me too well," Shayla said with a soft chuckle. She was glad to see her mother had perked up, that they were having a conversation that was normal. "Deedee felt it was a good idea that I had some sort of protection while I'm here, especially with the anniversary of the deaths coming up so quickly. I know it sounds crazy, but at least if I have someone looking out for me, I can be certain that no one can hurt me."

"It doesn't hurt that he's as good-looking as he is."

"Mom! What's gotten into you?"

"The one thing I would love to see before I leave this world is you with someone who makes you happy. Someone who's going to take care of you. Allow me to dream a little. I know how much you used to like Tavis, and I think he's a good guy."

Shayla wanted to remind her mother how Tavis had made his lack of feelings for her clear after Hayley's death, but she didn't bother. Their conversation was jovial and light. She didn't want to ruin the mood. She stroked her mother's hand then lifted it to her lips and softly kissed it. "One thing at a time," she said with a smile. "The most important thing is for you to know that there's no need to lose any sleep worrying about me. Let's worry about getting you better."

Her mother's eyelids began to flutter. They were getting heavy, and it seemed a struggle for her to keep them open. The nurse had told her that the pain medication caused drowsiness.

Shayla kissed her mother's hand again, saying, "I'll let you get some rest. I love you, Mom."

"I love you too, sweetheart."

Shayla went upstairs to her room, where she closed the door and pressed her back against it. She drew in a deep breath then finally let out the sob she'd been holding in. Seeing her mother like this was the hardest thing in the world. What she'd gone through with the murders and the scorn and the hate paled in comparison to the idea that she might be losing her mom.

"You're not going to lose her," she told herself. "You're going to be strong for her because that's what she needs. You're going to help her get through this."

Shayla glanced at her dresser. And frowned.

Her jewelry box...had it been moved?

Shayla moved forward, eyeing the box. It held only costume jewelry, nothing valuable. But still. She was certain that it had been closer to the corner of the dresser.

Closing her eyes, she shook her head. The stress was getting to her. She was imagining things.

With her eyes still closed, she started thinking about the night her life had changed. She had tried to flee the memories, but here she was, back in her old house and face-to-face with the reality she couldn't escape.

Opening her eyes, she went to the closet and

slowly opened the door. She'd thrown the teddy bear in there the other day, but had not bothered to look inside. Because inside, there were many memories she had tried to bury in the deep recesses of her mind. Now, as she turned on the light in the closet, she saw ribbons hanging from nails in the wall, countless trophies. All of her accolades from her world of dance. She and Hayley had been free-style dancers, and had competed for twelve years. It was something they'd both loved and done well at. They'd competed on teams as well as individually.

And when Hayley had failed to make the cut for the regional competition, everything had gone to hell. Hayley had complained about feeling unwell that day, her stomach bothering her. And she hadn't performed as well as she could have; that had been apparent to Shayla the moment she'd started her routine. But Shayla had been on point, doing her dance exercise to perfection. She'd secured a spot, and Hayley hadn't.

As the days had passed, Hayley's failure had seemed to make her more and more angry with Shayla. Shayla had tried to be patient with her, but Hayley had not been up to seeing any reason.

Then came the night of the party, and though they were talking, it was clear to Shayla that their relationship wasn't the same. She'd tried to make things normal between her and Hayley again, without success. But at least when she'd agreed to go to Lucas's party, she'd thought that things were finally on the mend between them.

Until Hayley had gotten into the car and started to go on and on about the competition again, and how Shayla thought she was so special because she'd made it and Hayley hadn't.

By the time Shayla had driven up to Lucas's place, she'd been in no mood to go to any party. Her best friend was saying things she simply couldn't understand. Had Shayla known that Hayley was going to go off the deep end over all of this, she would have forfeited her spot. It wouldn't have felt good for her to do it, but she would have done it. She wanted Hayley more than she wanted another trophy.

Shayla stifled a sob, hating this trip down memory lane. "Oh, Hayley. Why did you let that competition come between us? Did I do something wrong? Was there something I should have done instead? And now you're gone and we can never repair anything." Her voice ended on a croak.

She let the tears fall. Tears for her friend who had died. Tears for the animosity that had come between them before her death. Tears for her mother. Tears for herself and for what she'd lost.

Then she brushed the tears away and sucked in a deep breath. She couldn't wallow in pain over the past. She needed to move forward. She would never understand what had truly gotten into Hayley, and that wasn't how she wanted to remember her. She wanted to remember the smiling girl with the ridiculous-sounding half snort, half giggle that was totally infectious. She wanted to remember all the happiness she had shared with her best friend.

Chapter Six

Shayla's eyes flew open, instantly greeting the darkness of the room. For a moment, she didn't breathe. She felt disoriented and alarmed. Something had awakened her.

She lay still, concentrating on listening. And there it was again. A sound. Some sort of thump?

Her heart began to race. She was in her mother's room downstairs, her body folded into the armchair. She glanced toward her mother, who was snoring slightly as she slept. The IV beside the bed was dripping slowly, the monitor seemingly undisturbed. So what had awakened her?

Shayla got up, her legs cramping slightly as she stretched her body out from where she'd been curled for so long. Then she exited the den and started down the hallway. When she got to the living room, she saw the curtains by the patio door blowing gently. A draft?

No, she realized, stepping closer. The back door was open!

As fear took hold of her, she quickly whirled

around and tried to figure out what she could use as a possible weapon. Someone was in the house...

She rushed to the kitchen, hoping that no one was hiding there. Then she took the biggest knife from the butcher's block. Slowly, acting on instinct, she tiptoed to the back patio door. The curtains billowed with the light breeze.

Shayla drew in even, steady breaths, not wanting to make a sound. She tiptoed toward the patio door. As she got closer, she could hear a voice. A female?

She stepped up to the back door and hit the light switch to illuminate the backyard. And as she peered out, she saw Jennifer sitting at the patio table, her cell phone to her ear. Jennifer quickly threw a glance over her shoulder then lowered her phone.

A relieved sigh rushed out of Shayla's body. It was only the nurse. But why was she there? It was the middle of the night.

"Jennifer?"

The nurse got to her feet. Whomever she'd been talking to, she had quickly ended the call. "Sorry. Did I wake you?"

"Why are you here? Didn't you go home?"

Jennifer gave her an odd look. "Don't you remember I said I would stay later tonight because of how your mother was today? I know it was likely that she was just having a panic attack, but with her breathing difficulties during the day, I told you I'd stay."

Had she? Shayla couldn't remember. But the day had been a blur, with so much transpiring and the fear that her mother had taken a turn for the worse.

"Oh. I don't remember that. But I haven't even seen you throughout the evening."

"I checked in on your mother, and you were sleeping beside her, in the armchair. When I checked your mother's vitals, you didn't even budge. You were out cold."

"Oh. And how are her vitals?"

"They're back to normal. I think her episode today was stress related."

Jennifer's cell phone lit up. It was ringing, but on silent.

"You were talking to someone, weren't you?" Shayla asked. "I interrupted you."

"My boyfriend. You startled me, and I hung up on him."

"Yeah, I know the feeling."

"I'm sorry about that." Jennifer glanced at her phone's screen. "That's him calling back." She swiped to reject the call then typed out a text. When she was finished, Jennifer looked at her with concern. "You look a bit stressed yourself. Can I get you something? Maybe a sleeping pill might help?"

"No. I'm fine." She paused. "Good night."

"Good night. I hope you get some rest."

Shayla wandered through the living room and looked out the front window. Tavis's vehicle was there, as he'd promised he would be.

So he'd meant what he'd said. He would give her round-the-clock protection. Though at some point he needed to sleep.

Should she go out and offer him some food or a drink? Maybe a steaming cup of coffee?

She quickly dismissed the idea. He was an expert at protecting people; he certainly had to be prepared for long nights. Besides, she didn't want to see more of him than was necessary. It had already thrown her for a loop that he was back in her life, and she knew that however nice he was being to her now, he still blamed her to some degree for what had happened to Hayley. He was doing the right thing by her at this point because he was an honorable man, but he probably would be happy to see less of her as well.

With the nurse staying the night and her mother resting, Shayla headed upstairs to her room and crawled into her bed. Hopefully she could sleep the rest of the night without any distractions.

"Hey, Tavis," Griffin said into the phone. "Something's going on here."

Tavis, who was lying in his bed, quickly threw the covers off. It was four thirteen in the afternoon, but his room showed no sign of daylight due to his blackout curtains. He'd needed rest after being with Shayla for nearly twenty-four hours. And that was why Griffin was there at the house right now.

"What's going on?" Tavis asked, now wide awake.

"Shayla is on the move."

"Where's she going?"

"I just asked her, and she gave me the runaround. She exited the house and headed to her mother's car. That's when I approached her. You want me to give her the phone so you can ask her?"

"Yes. Put her on."

"Hold on."

Tavis heard the sound of shuffling as Griffin exited the vehicle. Then he could hear the faint sounds of Shayla's voice in the background as Griffin talked to her.

"Just going out for a little while."

"But you won't tell me where?"

"That's not necessary. I won't be gone long."

Griffin came back on the line. "She says she's going out and that she won't be long."

"Put her on the phone," Tavis said.

Next came Shayla's voice. "Hello?"

"Shayla, what's going on?"

"Nothing," she said, but her voice sounded a little strained.

"Where are you going?"

"I don't need protection every second of the day. I can go to the store, can't I?"

"Is that where you're going?" Tavis asked her. "To the store?"

She hesitated, and Tavis knew something else was going on. Something she didn't want to tell him.

"Wherever you need to go, I can take you. I'll be there in five minutes."

"Tavis," she protested. "You don't need to."

"Let me speak to Griffin," Tavis said.

Moments later, Griffin came back on the line.

"She's not gonna like this," Tavis said, "but block the driveway. Something's going on with her. I can hear it in her voice."

"I agree. She seems a bit on edge," Griffin said.

"Thanks for calling me. I'll be there soon."

SHAYLA WANTED TO SCREAM. She'd blown it. Blown her chance to escape and make the trip to Buffalo that she needed to make. She could call the sheriff to complain that she was being blocked in her driveway, but she didn't want to take it to that level. She just… She hoped she hadn't ruined the plan.

Tavis pulled up to the curb and exited his vehicle. He went over to Griffin's SUV and spoke for several seconds before the other man drove off. Tavis then turned his attention to where she sat on the front step. He stalked up the driveway, all six-foot-three muscular inches of him, and despite the look of irritation on his face, Shayla found herself reacting to his purely male presence.

"What's going on?" he asked her. "You know the deal is that I provide you round-the-clock protection."

"I just need to go somewhere." She got to her feet. "I can't tell you about it, and I don't need you following me."

Tavis's eyebrows shot up. "You can't tell me about it?"

"Maybe I have a romantic rendezvous lined up," she said, then immediately felt silly. Why on earth had she said *that*?

"You have a date?" Tavis asked doubtfully.

"That's such an impossible concept?" she asked, doubling down on her lie.

"Obviously not," Tavis said. "You're a very beautiful woman. But that's not what's going on here."

Shayla didn't want to think about the fact that he'd just said she was beautiful, or the fact that he knew she was lying.

"Wherever you want to go," Tavis went on, "I can take you there."

"You're going to ruin everything," Shayla mumbled.

Tavis's lips twisted. "Huh?"

Shayla exhaled sharply. How was she going to get out of this? She sucked at lying. And time was ticking. The call had come an hour ago, and she had expected to be in Buffalo by now.

"Tell me what's going on here," Tavis said.

A beat passed. Then two. And then Shayla let it spill. "I got a call. From Lucas."

An expression of stunned disbelief came across Tavis's face and his entire body went rigid. *"Lucas?"*

"I didn't want to tell you because… Because you're going to think that I've lied about everything. But he called me. Out of the blue. And he said that he needs to meet me."

"Lucas Carr?"

It was as much a shock for him as it had been for her. When she'd heard the voice, gravelly and faint, she hadn't been able to place it at first. And when he'd said that it was Lucas and he needed her help, she had been blown away.

"He said he knows I'm back in town, and that what happened on the night of the murders isn't what everyone says. He said he needs my help—help to clear his name." She paused. "I believe him. I always told you I never thought he killed anyone."

"And he wants you to go to Buffalo. To meet him."

"He can't very well show up in Sheridan Falls. He gave me an address. I already looked it up online. It's a house."

"And you were just gonna take off and go there without telling me?"

"He said to come alone. What did you want me to do?"

"I wanted you to tell me because you're sure as hell not going alone. I'll take you there."

"If I show up with anyone, it's going to spook him. He said if anyone else knows I'm meeting him, it could get him arrested."

"So you planned to go there alone." Tavis shook his head, disappointment evident in his eyes. "You thought that was safe?"

Shayla wasn't stupid. She'd considered the danger. But she'd asked him questions about their relationship, the party, and he'd answered them all. "I know there's a risk, but it's a house in the middle of a neighborhood. It's still day. If I can get answers about what happened, isn't that a good thing?"

Tavis gave her a pointed look. Then he said, "We're gonna take my car."

SHAYLA SAT HUGGING the passenger door and staring out the window with a conflicted expression as Tavis drove to the address in downtown Buffalo. He had left her to her thoughts, certain she felt bad about how everything had played out. It was beyond him that she had planned to drive to this address by herself, not fearing at all that she could be heading straight into danger.

Tavis's adrenaline was pumping. All these years he'd been looking for Lucas and, out of the blue, he had reemerged.

Shayla's cell phone rang. She glanced at the screen then at him. "It's Lucas."

"Answer it," Tavis told her.

"Hello?" Shayla said. "Yes, I'm on the way. I'll be there in…" She glanced at the GPS. "Seven minutes. Okay, see you soon."

"He's at the house?" Tavis asked once she ended the call.

"Yes."

Minutes later, they were off the highway and heading onto Niagara Street. They passed a fast-food restaurant and a pharmacy, then turned right after passing a grocery store. There were a lot of people milling about on this warm summer evening. This was the inner city, where there was more crime, and Tavis didn't like that Lucas had asked her to come here alone. The man was believed to have killed two people, and now he wanted to see her without anybody there to help her? How had Shayla not considered that Lucas might want to hurt her too? Though her quiet and pensive demeanor told him she was understanding that now.

He didn't want to give her a hard time, but he wanted her to understand that he was offering her protection for a reason. Someone wanted to hurt her; possibly kill her, if the threats were real. Once she'd gotten the request to go to a location in downtown Buffalo, she should have called him immediately.

Slowing, Tavis turned left. On the street corner, a few people were standing with their bicycles.

"It's not a desolate area, as you can see," Shayla suddenly said.

"True," Tavis agreed. But that didn't mean anything. People got hurt in the middle of crowds, in front of witnesses. You didn't always know where a bullet came from.

Tavis pulled up in front of a house. It took him a moment to read the number—thirty-seven—because the metal had faded due to the weather. "This is it."

It was dusk now, the sun dipping farther on the horizon every minute. Shayla reached for the door handle, but Tavis quickly put a hand on her arm. "Let me go out, have a look around."

"Okay," she said.

Tavis exited his vehicle, glancing all around as he did. Curious neighbors regarded him warily. He offered a small nod in the direction of the couple on the porch two houses over, trying not to look conspicuous. This was the kind of neighborhood where people would be curious as to who was showing up without cause.

He walked up to the front door and knocked. He was greeted by silence. He strained his ear against the door to listen, but heard no sound.

Hearing his pickup door open, he turned to see Shayla exiting the vehicle. "He's waiting for me," she said. "If you call out to him, he's probably going to run. Whatever we do, right now we do it together."

"Fine," Tavis said. "But you stick to my side."

She walked up the steps to meet him. "All I want to ask is that you give Lucas a chance. I know you're going to want to drag him to the authorities, but let's hear what he has to say. If he says he didn't kill Hayley and Jonathan, I believe him. I never believed he would do such a thing."

"I'm shocked that he's still in Buffalo. I thought he would've been far, far away from New York State by now." Some criminals took off to another continent and started a new life to evade the law. Lucas had apparently stuck around.

Shayla knocked on the door. Again, there was silence. She called out. "Lucas? It's me, Shayla."

No one answered.

Tavis tried the door. It opened. As he let it fall open fully, he met Shayla's gaze. She looked up at him and shrugged.

Tavis took the first step into the house. He looked around cautiously, seeing nothing but an empty hallway. On the right was a small, furnished living room. Directly ahead, he could see part of a kitchen. The house was quiet.

Turning around, Tavis nodded toward Shayla, letting her know that it was okay to enter.

Shayla followed him inside. She tiptoed up beside him, and Tavis could feel her energy. She was afraid.

His own heart was pumping, the hairs on the back of his neck standing at attention. Everything in his gut told him that something was off. Why would Lucas have her meet him here? And more importantly, where was he?

"Where is Lucas supposed to be?" Tavis whispered.

"He just said to come to this address. He didn't say anything else."

"Then where is he?" Tavis asked as he stepped farther into the small house. The wood floors creaked beneath their steps.

"Maybe he saw you, or heard you, and took off. I told you that I needed to come alone."

"That wasn't gonna happen."

As they headed toward the kitchen at the back of the house, a door suddenly flung open. A figure appeared, dressed in black. Tavis saw the shape of the gun and in the moments before it fired, had precious milliseconds to throw his body against Shayla's and force her to the floor. A bullet whizzed almost silently over their heads, lodging somewhere in the living room.

Shayla screamed. Tavis quickly shot to his feet, grabbing his gun from the holster beneath his jacket. He gave chase. The shooter, racing for the back door, turned and fired off another shot. It went high, landing in the wall above Tavis's head.

"Tavis!" Shayla screamed.

The shooter flung open the back door and rushed outside, firing another shot over his shoulder as he did.

Tavis had to duck to avoid getting hit.

"Nooo!" Shayla cried.

"Damn it!" Tavis ran to the back door and onto the dilapidated deck, saw the figure in black darting through the alleyway at the side of the house.

He wanted to sprint down the alley and catch up with the guy, but he couldn't leave Shayla. He turned and raced back to her. She was wincing, holding her elbow.

"Are you all right?" Tavis asked. He got onto the floor beside her. "Let me see your elbow."

Shayla partially extended her arm, moaning as she did. "It's just hurt. I don't think it's broken."

Tavis took her arm in his hand, gently checking for any damage. "It doesn't feel dislocated. I'm sorry. I had no choice but to knock you to the ground."

"Of course you didn't. He shot at us."

"He got away," Tavis said. "I couldn't go after him, not with you here."

"I think we spooked him."

Tavis looked at Shayla for a moment, dumbfounded. Did she not realize what had just happened? "Shayla, you must realize what happened here. Lucas lured you to this house. Not to give you information, but to get rid of you."

Her eyes bulged and her lips fell open. "No. That's not true. He wouldn't."

"But he did."

"That's because I didn't come alone. He freaked out. Probably thought you were going to take him to jail. He…he shot to scare us, so that he could get away."

Tavis placed both hands on Shayla's shoulders and looked her directly in the eye. "The person who came out of the bathroom was dressed in all black, right down to a ski mask. It wasn't Lucas suddenly scared because you showed up with someone else. That was someone prepared to kill and make a clean getaway."

Shayla's pupils seemed to jump as she registered his words. She shook her head slowly. "No. It… Lucas wouldn't do that. Why would he do that?"

"He even had a silencer on the gun to minimize the sound. You must understand now that if you had come here on your own, you would've been killed, right?" She didn't speak, as if unable to comprehend his words. "The threat to your life is very real. You have to take it seriously."

"I thought I was going to get answers. I even googled the address to make sure it was a safe location. It's a fairly public place. There are neighbors everywhere…"

"None of that matters when someone wants to kill you," Tavis told her.

She gasped then, finally understanding the gravity of the situation. "But I don't understand why he would want to kill me. After all this time?"

Tavis gathered her in his arms and pulled her to her feet. "I don't know either. But let's get out of here."

As Tavis led Shayla out of the house, he stopped short when he saw two young men standing at the foot of the walkway. Had they heard the shots? Likely not, because the shooter had used a silencer. But there was no guarantee.

"Hey, who are you guys?" one of the men asked, eyeing them suspiciously.

Tavis glanced at Shayla. Then she said, "I was

supposed to meet someone here. Maybe you know him?"

"Jenae?" the man supplied.

Though hearing the name hit him like a ton of bricks, Tavis did his best not to react.

"Jenae?" Shayla asked. "You know Jenae?"

"She was living there for a little while, but suddenly she took off."

"When?" Tavis asked.

"Hmm, about a week and a half ago—two," the second guy said around the lollipop in his mouth.

"What about Lucas?" Shayla asked.

"The guy she was living with? Shaker, that's what he went by."

His street name. Tavis asked, "You didn't know his real name?"

Both of the men shook their heads. "Only knew him as Shaker."

Tavis sauntered to the end of the walkway. "If you hear from Jenae or Shaker, tell them to call Tavis. They already have the number."

"Will do," the guy sucking the lollipop said. "Though I'm not sure if we'll ever see them again. She and Shaker took off real quick."

Chapter Seven

All Shayla wanted to do when she got home was go hug her mother and then slip into a warm bubble bath and stay there for a long while. She was relieved that the nurse had agreed to stay again for the night, because Shayla was so shaken by the events that had happened that she was in no proper position to care for her mother. She needed to decompress, take a hot bath and slip under the covers.

If you had come here on your own, you would've been killed...

Tavis's words reverberated in her brain as she sat in the bubble bath, wondering what she'd actually been thinking. Surely, she had to have known that going to see Lucas might be dangerous, but she'd completely pushed any thought of danger from her mind.

It had been hearing Lucas's voice, the way he'd desperately pleaded with her for help, that had her throwing caution to the wind.

I didn't do this. Everyone thinks I did. I can't return to Sheridan Falls without getting arrested. I need you to help me, Shayla. Please. Please help me clear my name. I can't go on like this anymore! You know how many people want me dead?

The plea had been earnest, heartfelt, and how could she have denied him? Especially when he'd gone on to explain that he'd had to live underground, hiding and watching his back—how that wasn't a life at all.

In her own way, she understood.

Had he really said all that just to get her to show up and meet him so he could kill her? Or had he started shooting because Tavis had showed up as well?

Shayla had had another idea; one Tavis hadn't agreed with. But it had occurred to her that maybe Lucas had set up extra security to make sure that she had come alone. Maybe he'd been working with someone else to protect him, and that person was the one who'd been hiding out at the house. Had Shayla gone there alone, the mystery man would have gotten word to Lucas and Lucas would have come to meet her. When she'd showed up with Tavis instead, the guy had panicked and come out shooting.

Tavis hadn't believed that for a second, and now as Shayla rethought the theory, she didn't believe it either.

Shayla eased her body lower into the tub so that her shoulders were covered by the bubbles and hot water. She didn't want to think about any of this anymore. All she knew was that someone had shot at her and Tavis.

At a house where Jenae had once lived.

Despite everything, that had been the biggest

shock of the day. The house she'd been sent to had very recently belonged to Jenae Wilkinson.

So what was the connection between her and Lucas?

And did one or both of them want her dead?

HALF AN HOUR after returning to Sheridan Falls, Tavis's blood was still pumping hard through his veins after pretty much coming face-to-face with a killer. Thank God the guy hadn't been a good shot, because he and Shayla could very well be dead right now. And they were no closer to finding Lucas.

"This case just got real," Griffin said. Tavis was sitting beside him in his Chevy Tahoe. "All these years later, it went from cold to hot."

"That it did, Griffin. That it did."

"You think that was actually Lucas at the house?"

"I'm not sure. I didn't get close enough to him to find out. If it is him, he wants Shayla dead. But why—and why now?"

Griffin lifted his coffee carafe and took a sip. "Are you going to report the shooting to the police?"

Tavis pursed his lips as he met Griffin's gaze. His friend knew him too well. "If I contact any of my former police colleagues about Lucas, they'll probably want to throw *me* behind bars. They don't want to hear anything about it. And you know Sheriff Thompson, he's not going to want to hear that I'm still looking for Lucas. I'll get the police involved when I find some concrete evidence."

Tavis's gaze wandered to Shayla's house. He had told her the same, that she shouldn't breathe a word of what had happened to the sheriff's department. What was the point? They were no closer to finding Lucas, and they couldn't give an accurate description of the shooter.

"Go home, Tavis," Griffin said. "I've got this. You know I'll make sure she's safe."

Tavis looked at his friend. "I know. I just… It's been a long day."

"Which is why you need to get some rest. I'm a phone call away. If anything happens, you know I'll reach out to you immediately."

"Thanks, Griffin." Tavis had some work to do at home anyway. Sleep would have to wait.

He exited Griffin's vehicle and was on his way. What did Jenae Wilkinson have to do with all of this?

Until just last week, Jenae had apparently lived at the address where someone had lured Shayla to kill her. According to Shayla, there was no reason that Jenae would want her dead. She'd been friendly with Jenae years ago, but not friends.

Tavis quickly pulled into his driveway then slammed on the brakes. He needed to dive into his files to see if he could find a connection between Jenae and Lucas. Something he'd overlooked before, or a connection he had failed to make.

"Why can't you just let this go?" Sheriff Thompson had asked him late last year when Tavis had tried to get him to look into a lead about where Lucas could have been. At the time, Tavis had received an anonymous message about Lucas living on the Big Island under an alias. He'd wanted the Sheridan Falls' police resources to track the person down and verify if it was indeed Lucas. But Sheriff Thompson had wanted none of it.

Ultimately, Tavis had gone around Thompson and gotten the information from Deputy Mike Jenkins. It hadn't been Lucas after all.

Apparently he'd been in Buffalo all this time.

Tavis hurried into his modest two-story house. He took the stairs two at a time to the second level, then went into the spare bedroom that he'd turned into his war room. There was no bedroom set in this room, but a desk and table and cabinets with various files. In this room, he had everything to do with the murders.

Tavis stood in front of the wall on which he'd erected a large whiteboard. It had all the visuals corresponding to the case. In the center was a picture of Hayley and one of Jonathan. From there he had lines drawn toward Lucas, and also Shayla, and the other friends who'd been at the party that night. There were family members and more friends from school connected to the pair, with his notes detailing useful points and questions.

He kept his detailed notes in his binder and files, which included the interviews he'd done over the years. But no one had given him anything useful. People offered speculations, theories, and the belief that Lucas was a no-good bad boy who had likely changed his identity and was living undetected somewhere.

Tavis moved to the wall. Jenae Wilkinson had been Alex Thompson's girlfriend, and had left town not long after the murders. She'd headed clear across the country to Oakland, California, for college, and after her degree had returned to Upstate New York. She and Alex had gotten married and had settled in Buffalo, but they'd divorced two years ago.

Something about his conversations with Jenae had always left him unsettled. Her story was both vague and detailed. With what he'd learned today, Tavis wondered if she'd deliberately kept critical information from him.

According to her, she'd been at the party but so high that she hadn't been paying attention to anything. She'd been drinking and smoking pot. Sure, there might've been a few squabbles, but she'd left long before anything serious had happened. She knew nothing.

That had been her initial story. Vague. And then she'd somehow remembered some details with stunning clarity. So much so, that Tavis didn't believe her. His years as a cop had taught him that when suspects were too vague or too detailed, they were most likely lying. And when their stories changed, it was pretty much a guarantee that they weren't telling the truth.

Given her initial lack of recall, when Jenae had suddenly offered Tavis a timeline that was very exact, he'd heard her out but had been wary. According to her, at eight thirty, she'd arrived at the party. By nine o'clock, she'd already had two drinks and had been smoking weed. By nine thirty, she was starting to lose her senses. By ten, she wasn't feeling well and had asked Alex to take her home. At ten fifteen, she'd been crawling into bed. She hadn't been sure if Alex had gone back to the party. Maybe he had? But according to Jenae, Alex had told her that he'd left the party before anything major happened.

For someone so vague on other details, she'd come up with a pretty specific timeline that had Tavis wondering if she'd created that story. But at the end of the day, he hadn't believed that Jenae was involved in the murders.

Now, he wasn't so sure anymore. He wanted to talk to her again. But to do that, he needed to find her.

Tavis picked up his cell phone and called Deputy Mike Jenkins. He answered after the first ring.

"Deputy Jenkins."

"Hey, Mike. It's Tavis."

"Oh, hey, Tavis. How are you?"

"I'm okay. But I have a favor to ask."

"Of course you do. What is it? I can't guarantee I can help."

Tavis knew the routine already. Mike didn't want to cross certain lines. He didn't want to push the rules or break them, but Tavis still reached out to him on many occasions to see if he would do just that.

"Jenae Wilkinson," Tavis said. "I'm trying to find her."

"Didn't you ask me this last year?"

"Well, that was a year ago. I wasn't able to find her then. But I've had this feeling, call it a hunch, and I feel the need to follow up on it."

"You're killing me, man."

"Last year I wanted to talk to her and go through her statement again. I've spent some time reconfirming the statements of most of the people I interviewed. But I've been looking at what she told me. I find it suspect." He didn't want to tell Jenkins about the house in Buffalo…not yet.

"What's talking to Jenae going to do for the case? You think she killed Hayley and Jonathan and disposed of their bodies?"

"I'm not saying that. But I want to talk to her again. I want to see if she's got more to tell me now than she did before. She could've been afraid the first time. You know how it goes. Witnesses change their stories all the time."

"All right, Tavis," Deputy Jenkins grudgingly agreed. "I'll see what I can do."

Chapter Eight

"Come on, Mom," Shayla said, helping her mother to sit up on the bed. "I know you're weak, but let's get you up. Let's take a short walk to the kitchen."

"Oh, sweetheart. I don't know."

"You need to get a little exercise in. I can't begin to say that I know what you're going through, but I know that you need to move your legs and your arms. I'm with you. I've got you."

Her mother began to shift her legs over the side of the bed, and Shayla helped her. Then she wrapped her arms around her mother's torso and held her, guiding her to the floor.

"Are you okay?" Shayla asked.

Her mother was unsteady on her feet, but after a moment, she said, "Yes. I'm okay."

The pole with the IV was attached to her arm, and Shayla grabbed it so they could walk with it down the hallway. "I am glad that you're here. Maybe you're what I need for this fight."

"I know that I am. There's so much I have yet to do, Mom. And I need you here for all of it."

"I hope that soon you'll find someone nice in

your life. Someone to take care of you and give you babies."

Shayla wasn't sure if that was in the cards for her, but she agreed with her mother to make her feel better. "I'd love nothing more than to give you lots of grandchildren. But you've gotta be here to see them. Deal?"

"Deal." They walked slowly, her mother taking one careful step at a time through the hallway. And then the doorbell rang. They were crossing the threshold into the living room, and Shayla guided her mother to the sofa. "Sit here for a second, Mom. Let me get the door."

Shayla hurried to the front door and opened it. The nurse was out doing some errands, and Shayla didn't expect that it was her. She looked through the peephole, and seeing Sheriff Thompson, she was instantly alarmed. Had he heard about what had happened yesterday? She quickly opened the door.

"Sheriff Thompson," she said, a hint of a question in her voice. "Is everything okay?"

"Hello, Shayla." He tipped his Stetson toward her. "I'm here to make sure you're okay."

Shayla swallowed. "Oh?"

"I hear you took your car in to be cleaned up. My son Chase told me."

"Yes." Shayla smiled softly, relaxing. "I didn't know that that was his shop. He promised he'd fix my car up for me. I should be able to get it maybe by tomorrow."

"He took a picture of the threat written on your windshield and sent it to me. It was pretty ballsy of whoever did it. Just wondering if there's anything else that's happened. Any other thing making you feel unsafe?"

For a moment, Shayla wondered if the sheriff knew about what had happened in Buffalo yesterday. But how could he? Tavis wasn't going to say anything, and she'd agreed to keep silent about it as well. "Only Donny a couple of days ago," she told him. "Since then, things have been okay."

"Is that Sheriff Thompson?" her mother called out.

"Yes, ma'am. Glad to hear your voice."

"Thank you," her mother returned. "I'd come to the door, but I'm not properly dressed."

"That's okay, ma'am," the sheriff said.

Shayla was glad to hear that her mother had summoned the strength to call out to the sheriff, even if she wasn't able to rise to her feet to come to the door. She was in her nightgown, and not dressed for company anyway.

"I was just helping my mother take a little walk around the house. She's still very weak," Shayla told Sheriff Thompson.

"That's okay. I'm not staying. I just wanted to reiterate that if you feel unsafe at all, or if anything happens that's bothersome, please do call me." He withdrew a business card and handed it to her. "You don't need Tavis nor his sidekick, Griffin, tailing you and probably getting you into worse trouble."

"What do you mean 'getting me into worse trouble'?"

"Tavis… I don't know what it is about him, but trouble finds him. He's the type who gets himself mixed up where he shouldn't. Let me just leave it at that. You have a problem with anyone in this town, call me. I'm the sheriff. I'll take care of it."

The sheriff would no doubt see what had happened yesterday as proof of his point about Tavis, though what had happened hadn't been his fault. Shayla tapped the card against her palm. "Okay. Thank you, Sheriff Thompson. But I'm hoping that the incident with Donny was the last of it."

"Me too."

The sheriff turned, about to leave, but quickly pivoted back on his heel. "By the way, I'm not sure if you're aware, but tomorrow there's a vigil for Hayley and Jonathan. It happens every year on the anniversary of their deaths."

"Yes, I heard about it."

"I'm wondering if maybe you shouldn't go, in case you were planning on it. If someone here is angry enough to hurt you, might be best you not give them the opportunity."

"You think I should stay away? If people know I'm here and I don't go, maybe that will give them *more* reason to be upset."

"But you don't want to push your luck, now, do you? I know you didn't have anything to do with killing Hayley and Jonathan. And in their hearts, the people in this town know it too. But that won't stop people from giving you a hard time."

A few harsh words Shayla could handle. Keeping safe from someone who wanted her dead was another matter. Was it Jenae? Or Lucas?

"Don't get me wrong," the sheriff went on. "Many

are still angry. They either think that Lucas was defending your honor where Hayley was concerned, or that you know where he went. So, all things considered, there could be some bad blood at the vigil that you might want to avoid."

"I'll take the advice under advisement," Shayla said. "I didn't come back here for the vigil. I came here for my mom."

Sheriff Thompson nodded. "You take care now."

"You too."

AFTER SHAYLA GOT her mother back into bed and once the nurse returned, she went to get her phone. That's when she saw that she had missed a call from Tavis. She called him back and he answered after the first ring.

"Hey, Shayla. Did you get my message?"

"No, I just saw that you called, so I figured I would call you back. I noticed that you're not outside."

"That's why I was calling. To let you know that I'll be on my way soon. I was pretty much up all night going through my files, trying to see if there's something I missed. I still can't find a connection between Jenae and Lucas."

"And I don't know one either. They knew each other, but they weren't friends."

"I assume you called the number Lucas called you from."

"Yes, and it's out of service now."

"Figures," Tavis said, and Shayla could hear the frustration in his voice. "Let's forget about that for now. How are you today?"

"Uh, okay. In some ways, yesterday seems surreal. Like it was a dream."

"And how's your elbow?"

"Much better. I took a long hot bath last night, and a painkiller. I'll live."

"Griffin just texted to tell me that the sheriff was at your house."

"Yeah. Sheriff Thompson came by. He wanted to see how I was doing, and at first I wondered if he knew about yesterday. But he came by to check on me, and let me know that I should be in touch with him if there are any problems or threats. He ended up telling me that I should probably stay away from the vigil tomorrow, considering someone wants to do me harm."

"Really?"

"Yeah. I guess it makes sense. But I doubt Lucas will show up here. Anyone else at the vigil will probably give me dirty looks. Dirty looks, I can deal with."

"I agree, I don't think he'll show up here either." Tavis paused. "I've been searching for Jenae online, but I can't find any information on her. I know she ended up marrying Alex Thompson. I've seen some pictures of the two of them on his social media, as if they're still a happy couple. Have you been in touch with her online?"

"No," Shayla said. "When I left, I basically had to close all my social media accounts because of the hate. I kept in touch with a few people via phone and texting, but she wasn't one of them."

"I might track down Alex, see what he can tell me. I wonder if she's always had no social media presence, or if this is something new."

"You checked under Thompson, her married name?" Shayla asked.

"Yes, I checked both her maiden name and married name."

"I can ask my cousin if she has a way to reach her. They were both dating the Thompson boys, so maybe they stayed in touch."

"That'd be great," Tavis said. "You can let me know when I see you later."

"Sure thing."

When Shayla ended the call with Tavis, she punched in Deedee's number. "Hey, cuz," Deedee greeted her, a smile in her voice. "What's up?"

"Nothing much. Oh, my mom's doing a bit better. We went for a walk around the house earlier."

"That's great," Deedee said. "Tell her I'll be by to see her again soon. And my parents are coming back from North Carolina later this week, so they'll be visiting her then."

Shayla was looking forward to reuniting with her aunt and uncle, whom she hadn't seen in years. "I was talking to Tavis, and he had a question. He's trying to reach Jenae Wilkinson. I told him maybe you'd know how to get in touch with her?"

"Why does he want to reach her?"

For a moment, Shayla considered telling Deedee what had happened yesterday, but she didn't want to get into that right now. "Sounds like he wants to go over something she told him about the night of the murders. I'm not sure."

"Last I heard, Jenae and Alex broke up and Alex

came back to Sheridan Falls. I don't know what happened to Jenae."

"You don't have a number for her? Did you guys ever stay in touch?"

"We stayed in touch for a little while. Here and there, off and on. I'm sure the number I have for her is old, but I can try it."

"Oh, that'd be great. If you reach her, let me know."

"I will. Now, what are you going to do about tomorrow and the vigil?"

Shayla filled her cousin in on the fact that the sheriff had dropped by and ultimately told her he didn't think it would be a good idea for her to attend the vigil.

"I'm inclined to agree with him," Deedee said.

"I don't know if it's because everyone's telling me not to go, or because I feel I should be able to grieve for Hayley since I did nothing wrong. But I think I want to go. What time is it being held?"

"Two o'clock. At the school. It's always at the school because that's where their bodies were found. But, Shayla, I don't think you should go. It's a bad idea."

The more people didn't want her to go, the more she *did* want to go. There was no doubt she had a stubborn streak, and hadn't she let the townsfolk control her enough already?

"I hear you," Shayla said. "I'll make up my mind in the morning."

HOLDING A MUG of coffee, Shayla approached Tavis in his vehicle where he was parked outside of her house. She went over to the driver's side of his GMC Sierra and he lowered the window.

Smiling, she passed him the coffee. "Black with two sugar."

"Thank you. You didn't have to."

"It was no trouble. But…I tried to make a lasagna for you, figuring you were likely hungry, but I ruined it. I was wondering if maybe you feel up to taking a drive to Deedee's restaurant. I can treat you to a meal. And you can talk to Deedee about Jenae."

Tavis perked up. "She knows something?"

"I'm not sure, but I talked to her about Jenae, and she said she has some news. She doesn't want to share the news over the phone or via text. She wants to talk in person."

"Definitely, we can go over there. Now?"

"Just let me grab my purse."

A SHORT WHILE LATER, Tavis and Shayla were entering 24-Hour Breakfast and More. The hostess brought them to an available booth and placed two menus on the table in front of them.

"Your waitress will be with you shortly," the red-haired teenager said.

No sooner than the hostess walked away, a woman with short black hair began to approach their table. But fast on her heels was Deedee. "I've got this table, Amber," Deedee said, flashing the woman a bright smile.

"Oh…okay."

"This is my cousin, Shayla," Deedee explained. "And my friend Tavis."

"Nice to meet you both," Amber said, then sauntered off.

Deedee slid into the booth, beside Shayla. "Hey, Tavis. Good to see you."

"Good to see you too, Deedee."

Deedee glanced around before saying in a lowered voice, "You're trying to reach Jenae?"

"Yes," Tavis told her.

"Why?"

"It's about my cousin's murder. I want to verify a couple of the things she told me."

"After all this time?" Deedee asked. "What could she say now that could possibly help you?"

"Maybe she knows more than she ever told me," Tavis said. "I have my reasons for wanting to speak to her. Do you have a way to reach her?"

Deedee sighed softly. "I wasn't able to contact her directly. The number I had for her is out of service. But I talked to someone who does still talk to her. She conveyed the message that you wanted to reach her, and Jenae said that she has nothing more to tell you and she doesn't want anybody bothering her about the past."

Tavis frowned. "So she won't talk to me?"

"It sounds like she's a bit afraid," Deedee admitted. "Her marriage with Alex ended on bad terms. Like, really bad terms. She doesn't want him getting wind of where she is."

"I would never breach that confidence."

"I'm sure, but I can understand her hesitation. Maybe if you give me the specific questions you want to ask, I can forward them?" Deedee suggested.

Tavis shook his head. "No. That won't work. What I will do is give you my number. Tell her friend to pass along the message that I'd really like to hear from her. If she calls me, then we can talk."

"Okay," Deedee agreed. "Fair enough."

Shayla asked, "Did she ever say anything bad about me, Dee?"

"Not that I'm aware of. Why?"

"Just wondering," Shayla said. "So many people didn't like me. I don't know if Jenae was one of them."

Deedee shrugged. "If she ever said anything, it wasn't to me."

"And what about her and Lucas?" Shayla went on. "I don't remember them being friends, but maybe they were?"

Deedee looked between Shayla and Tavis, her eyes narrowing. "Why, what are you thinking?"

"I've been thinking about everyone who was at the party, and whether or not someone might be inclined to protect Lucas," Tavis answered. "I know you were there, but you left early, right?"

"I did," Deedee said.

"Do you remember what time?" Tavis asked.

Deedee's mouth fell open, but she didn't answer right away. "I don't exactly remember. That was nine years ago."

"But when you left, was Jenae still there?" Tavis pressed.

"I…I honestly don't remember. Maybe she left before me…?" Deedee's voice ended on a question. "I'm not really sure what you're getting at."

"Something happened…" Shayla began. It was time to fill her cousin in. "Yesterday—"

"Someone contacted Shayla," Tavis interjected.

"This person suggested that Jenae had possibly helped Lucas nine years ago."

"What?" Deedee couldn't hide her shock. "Who contacted you?"

Shayla looked to Tavis, who clearly didn't want her to tell Deedee about their trip to Buffalo yesterday. When he didn't speak, she did. "Someone called me. Said that Lucas and Jenae were connected..."

"Which is why I'm exploring all angles," Tavis said. "If I can talk to Jenae, she can answer these questions."

Deedee shook her head. "I don't know about that. I think Hayley and Jonathan were the last two people at the party, and that's when something went wrong. Lucas killed them, then freaked out and took off."

"Maybe there's no connection," Tavis admitted, "but I don't want to leave any stone unturned."

"I'm sure Deedee will do what she can to help," Shayla said, offering her cousin a smile. "If she can get a message to Jenae, great." She turned to Tavis. "I promised you a meal." She opened the menu. "Do you know what you want to eat?"

Tavis glanced at the menu. "I'll have a Philly cheesesteak sandwich. To go."

"Sure thing," Deedee said, her tone sounding clipped. She got out of the booth and headed toward the kitchen.

"You upset my cousin," Shayla said.

"I've got to ask questions, Shayla. If I don't ask questions, I won't get answers."

"But you made it sound like you were doubting her." Shayla could see the sheriff's point about Tavis.

He was like a dog with a bone, unwilling to give it up. But there was no point upsetting people when you needed their help. "And why didn't you want me to tell her about yesterday?"

"I'd prefer we keep that to ourselves for now. Until we learn more, I don't want word about that getting out."

"She wouldn't tell anyone."

"And she definitely won't if she doesn't know."

Shayla frowned. Tavis was being very hardheaded about this. "You seem upset," she said to him.

"I'm frustrated," he told her. "I know that someone knows something. Someone must. All these years, someone must've heard something."

"I know you want to solve this case. And God knows, I do too. Hayley was your cousin and my best friend. But…what if you can't? What if there are no answers?"

"You still believe that, after yesterday? Lucas contacted you. For the first time in nine years, he's back on the radar."

"But what if he disappears again, this time for good? This case might never be solved."

"I won't accept that. I can't live with that. I am going to solve this case, Shayla. Whether it's now, or five years from now. I'm going to get the answers that my family deserves."

Chapter Nine

*I'm really sorry. I don't feel well, but another nurse
will be coming in this morning.*

Shayla reread the text, stunned. She could accept that
the nurse wasn't feeling well. But why wouldn't she
have the decency to call?

Shayla pressed the phone icon to dial Jennifer's
number.

"Hello?" Jennifer sounded hoarse.

"Sorry to call you," Shayla began, "but I figured
it's easier to have a short conversation rather than
keep texting back and forth. I'm sorry to hear you're
not feeling well. Is this other nurse coming in for
eight?"

"Yes. She'll be there in the next half hour. I'll be
back tomorrow or maybe the next day. As long as I
shake this bug."

"Obviously, take the time you need to get well,"
Shayla told her, her irritation fading. If Jennifer was
sick, that wasn't good for her mother.

"I'm really sorry."

"No need to apologize." At least Jennifer had corresponded with her this time. She'd seemed perfectly fine last night, but sickness could come on instantly. She only hoped that whatever Jennifer had wasn't something that would affect her mother.

"Get well," Shayla told her.

"I will."

THE REPLACEMENT NURSE, Melanie, was an older woman who was efficient and aloof. She set about making oatmeal for her mother's breakfast, and after she'd eaten, Melanie got her up and out of bed. Again, her mother took a walk around the house, and Shayla was glad. Hopefully every day she'd get stronger and stronger.

While Melanie cared for her mother, Shayla spent some time online answering business emails and going through the orders.

A few of the emails she received were complaints. One large order for a dance team had not been delivered on schedule.

Before calling the supplier herself, Shayla called Lyndsay, her assistant manager, to see if the problem had been addressed.

"I'm already on it," Lyndsay told her. "There was a backlog, but the supplier is rushing the order and giving us a discount because of the delay. I'm going to pass the discount on to the customer."

"Good," Shayla said. "Keep me posted."

"I will. Look, don't worry about the store. I'm taking care of everything."

Shayla exhaled softly. "Thank you. I know you're

completely capable of handling things while I'm away."

When Shayla had decided to move the business online, Lyndsay would come to her house for the day, where they'd both work together, go through the orders and catalog the inventory delivered to her place. Lyndsay knew every aspect of the business. Dazzle Dance Designs was in good hands.

"Spend time with your mother," Lyndsay said. "How is she, by the way?"

"She seems stronger. She's been up and walking around. With some help, but still."

"I'm praying for her. And for you."

"Thank you."

"And what about you? Are you safe?"

Shayla's eyes ventured to the back of her bedroom door where her purses hung on a hook. She frowned, noticing that an older brown purse was now on the top. She hadn't touched that purse in ages. How was it on top?

"Shayla?" Lyndsay prompted.

"Um, yeah," Shayla said. "I've been safe." Maybe the purse had always been there and she wasn't remembering correctly. That had to be the case.

A beat passed. Then Lyndsay said, "I didn't want to tell you this, but obviously you need to know. An email came in to the store's account. Someone said that if you know what's good for you, you won't go to the vigil."

"When did you get that email?"

"This morning."

Shayla bit down on her bottom lip. "All right, thanks for telling me."

"You know I'm worried about you. Maybe you shouldn't go."

Shayla felt a spurt of anger. How tough this person was, anonymously threatening her. Lucas? That didn't feel right. He had called her and announced himself, so why send anonymous emails? Whoever had a problem with her, they should just make it known. She was tired of dealing with this.

"I have someone who's protecting me," Shayla said.

"What?" Lyndsay sounded shocked. "Like a bodyguard?"

"An old friend. Yes, he offers bodyguard services, and he's watching out for me. So I'm okay. Please don't worry about me."

"Well, I'm glad to hear that, but please stay in touch. Let me know that things are going well."

"I will."

As Shayla ended the call with Lyndsay, she contemplated calling the sheriff to let him know about this latest email threat. But he would just reiterate that she shouldn't go to the vigil.

Instead, Shayla headed outside. Tavis had been there this morning, not having taken a break since last night. He looked at her with concern as she approached the vehicle.

She got into the passenger seat. "I got some news. My assistant in Florida, who runs my e-store with me, told me that an email threat came in again. Someone who doesn't want me to go to the vigil."

"Were you planning to go?" Tavis asked.

Shayla squared her shoulders. "Yes. I am."

"Good. Because I plan to be there as well. That way I can have eyes on you as opposed to having Griffin come to the house to watch you."

Shayla smiled. "Perfect."

Back in the house, she called Deedee. "I hope you have the afternoon off as we discussed yesterday," Shayla said before Deedee could speak.

"You're not going to the vigil, are you?" Deedee asked.

"I am," Shayla said with resolve in her voice. "I'm in town, why shouldn't I?"

"You've already had a threat left on your car and a gun pulled on you. I think the last thing you should do is show your face at the vigil and give someone a chance to hurt you."

If only her cousin knew what had happened in Buffalo. But Shayla was certain that she'd be fine today, with her plan to stay at the back and observe. Besides, there was no way Lucas was going to show his face at the vigil.

"I know," she said. "But if people know I'm in town and I don't go, they'll have something to say, won't they? So I'm gonna go, stay at the back. Wear a hat. Try to remain unseen. And I would really like it if you'd go with me."

"Considering how stubborn you are, I made arrangements to have my shift at work covered. But I'm not happy about this."

"You'll be happy to know that Tavis will also be at the vigil, so it works out anyway. Otherwise he was going to have to call someone in to replace him to watch me at the house. Now he doesn't have to."

"You have this all worked out," Deedee said somewhat sourly.

"It's eleven thirty now, so that gives you a couple of hours to get here. I think we should leave here at one thirty to get to the school."

"Why do you have to be so stubborn?" Deedee asked her. "I think you're asking for trouble. Stay with your mother and leave the town to do what it always does. You don't need to be there."

Deedee sounded more concerned about the threat than she had before. "You must think someone's really going to hurt me?"

"Why take any chances?"

Had Deedee heard something? In a town like this, Shayla wouldn't be surprised. With her insistence that she not go to the vigil, Shayla wondered if there was something Deedee wasn't telling her. Or was she just being excessively cautious?

Of course, her cousin was the type to be excessively cautious, whether fearing sharks or rollercoasters. Maybe Deedee was simply worrying that the worst would happen.

"I'm gonna go," Shayla said. "If you don't want to pick me up, Tavis can give me a ride there. Just let me know."

"I'll pick you up," Deedee said grudgingly. "And I'll be there early enough so that Tavis can tail us to the vigil. That's the one thing I'm happy about—that he'll be there. Though, hopefully, he no longer thinks I'm lying about the night of the murders."

"He does tend to push hard," Shayla said. "But he doesn't think you're lying. He's just…determined to get answers."

"He could have fooled me. But I do understand. He lost his cousin."

"See you at one thirty?" Shayla said.

"See you at one thirty."

THE VIGIL WAS to start at two, and at exactly one fifty-five, Deedee pulled her car up in front of the school. The crowd had already gathered on the grass, balloons and candles in hand.

"That's a lot of people," Shayla commented.

"They pretty much shut down the town so everyone who wants to attend can. Two in the afternoon—"

"The exact time that dog walker found their bodies under the tarp at the back of the school by the dumpster," Shayla supplied.

Shayla gazed out at the crowd, nerves tickling her stomach.

"We don't have to do this," Deedee said to her.

"Yes, I do. I'm not here for anyone in this town. I'm here for myself. For Hayley and Jonathan."

Behind them, Tavis pulled his vehicle to a stop. "And my personal bodyguard has arrived." He'd been on a call when Deedee had driven off from her mother's house, so was delayed by a few minutes. "Which was your idea, by the way. So, no need to worry."

Deedee cut her eyes at her. Shayla offered her a tentative smile, then looked in the visor's mirror and adjusted the baseball cap on her head. Satisfied that her identity was adequately obscured, she opened the door. Deedee followed suit.

Together, Shayla and Deedee walked slowly toward the crowd. Shayla didn't want to get too close to the group. She wanted to linger at the back; be part of the throng of people, but safely away from them. With everyone facing the family members who were standing on the school steps at the front, Shayla didn't expect anyone would be spotting her in the crowd.

And it did seem as if much of Sheridan Falls was there. She recognized some of the faces as they turned to look in her direction. Chase was standing with his wife, Lisa, and his brother, Alex. Graham Knight, who'd been one of Jonathan's best friends. Alisha Macklin and Kelly DuPont, who'd been on the cheer squad. Almost all of the football team from years before was in attendance, many of them looking visibly older, some not so much. More women who'd been on the cheerleading squad. Other athletes. Molly from the coffee shop.

Shayla stopped walking. She stood behind a taller man she didn't recognize, hoping that she would melt into the crowd. She looped arms with her cousin.

Katie Harrison, who looked almost exactly the same as she had when she'd been a cheerleader, right down to her fiery red hair, was walking toward them with extra balloons. Shayla glanced away, not meeting her gaze.

"Hey, Deedee," Katie said. "Here are some balloons."

Deedee took them, and passed one to Shayla as Katie continued through the crowd.

The sound of someone clearing their throat reverberated through the microphone. Shayla looked to the front.

"Everyone with candles, please light them now," Eric, Jonathan's father, said.

People in the crowd took a moment to light their candles, some sharing the flame with those around them.

"Thank you all for coming today," Eric continued. "Once again, we are marking the grim milestone of Jonathan's and Hayley's passing. Of their *murders*. And, sadly, their killer has not been brought to justice."

Hayley's mother, Victoria, was weeping. Her hair was a thick afro now as opposed to the permed straight style that Shayla remembered. The afro looked good on her.

The tear-filled eyes did not.

She was holding the teddy bear that Shayla remembered all too well. Hayley'd had to sleep with it every night. Even when they went away for dance competitions, she'd brought that bear with her. It was her good luck charm, she'd always said.

Eric hugged his wife, Maria, comforting her as she also openly grieved. "People say time heals all wounds," Eric began, "but I can tell you that's not true. Each year, the pain cuts a little deeper knowing our precious son is still gone. That he's never coming back. Some days it feels like a dream and I think I'm going to wake up and he's going to be in his bed clutching one of those trains he loved so much, but it never happens."

"It's still like it happened yesterday," Maria said, holding her hand against her heart. "I'll never see my son play college football at Kent State as he was going to. I'll never see him married. There have been days I haven't wanted to go on."

Jonathan's younger sister, Emily, hugged her mother. There were more tears. It was hard to watch.

"I want to thank each and every one of you who has been supportive of us over the years," James, Hayley's father, said to the crowd. "My Hayley didn't deserve this, and neither did Jonathan. And while the pain is as deep as it is, I know it would be lessened if the killer could be brought to justice."

He looked through the crowd, seeming to find Shayla and stare her down. Shayla squirmed on the spot. Had he actually seen her? Or was he just looking in her general direction?

"I know this case can be solved," James went on. "And I know that someone in this town has answers. Think hard, think about what you know, what you remember. And if you've been keeping anything to yourself because of fear, take this time to do the right thing."

He was definitely looking in Shayla's direction. Deedee elbowed her. "You know he's talking to you."

Shayla said nothing. She wiped at the tear that was rolling down her cheek. She wanted to go forward and speak, say something on Hayley's behalf. Yet she knew she couldn't.

But others did. Friends and family went up and

relationships end and two people who loved each other no longer communicate. I was going to ask if you had a way for me to reach her, I wouldn't mind saying hi."

"Can't help you."

Shayla nodded. She lowered her gaze as people passed, not wanting anyone else to recognize her. "Well, it was nice running into you. But as I'm sure you know, my mom is sick. And I really do need to get back to her."

"Sure thing," Alex said. "See you around then, sometime."

"See you around," she said, then looped arms with Deedee's and hurried with her cousin toward the car.

TAVIS WOULD TYPICALLY be standing at the front of the vigil with his cousin and his aunt and uncle, but instead he sat in his vehicle, eyeing the gathering. He was watching for any threat to Shayla, of course. But he was also taking a look at the crowd from a different vantage point—as an investigator, not a mourner. He had his camera with him, and he was snapping shots of everyone so that he could examine them later.

In past years, he had mentally taken note of all the faces. Pretty much everyone in attendance had been people he'd known from the town. Yet he'd always looked for someone he didn't recognize, or someone who seemed fidgety or somehow out of place. He'd never specifically found anyone who'd been acting suspiciously, and he'd left each vigil with a sense of hopelessness. Because he was waiting for some break, something to happen, that would change the course of his investigation. But each year, he'd gotten nothing.

He slinked down his vehicle as Deputy Mike Jenkins walked from the grass toward the sidewalk. The deputy's cruiser was parked across the street from Tavis's pickup, but the man didn't stop and acknowledge Tavis, which was exactly as he wanted it right now. He wanted to scope out the dispersing crowd.

Sheriff Thompson was on the other side of the school, also watching the crowd. So was another deputy, Deputy Holland. The sheriff's department always came out for every vigil, allegedly doing what Tavis was now—but Tavis wasn't convinced that they were searching the crowd for clues. He figured they were in attendance to show their respect, nothing more. After all, Sheriff Thompson believed that Lucas was gone and never coming back because he would be too stupid to return to the town.

Tavis didn't disagree. Lucas had to know that returning to a small town like Sheridan Falls would be the same as walking into any police station and asking to be arrested.

Again, Tavis marveled at the fact that Lucas was in Buffalo. Had he been there all this time, or had he recently returned there?

Two people who were not at the vigil were Lucas's aunt and uncle, Rosita and Andrew Carr. They'd gone to the first one, and had been chased from the event. Just as Shayla had been. Even now, while they still lived in the town, they pretty much kept to themselves. They'd gotten some death threats in the beginning too, though Tavis had heard that the threats had died down after a few months. Maybe people realized that Rosita and Andrew were no more responsible for Lucas's actions than anyone else in Sheridan Falls. They'd taken in a troubled teen and had never imagined that he would kill two people and shame their names.

Tavis glanced to his left as a black sedan drove by. Speak of the devil, he saw Lucas's aunt in the passenger seat. Rosita and Andrew had come to the vigil after all.

But he didn't think they had exited their car, because he hadn't spotted them in the crowd. Maybe they'd been watching from a distance? Or were they simply driving by the school at this moment?

Looking from the Carr vehicle and back to the crowd, someone caught Tavis's attention. A person in a baseball cap on the far side of the field. Quickly picking up his camera, he zoomed in and took a photo. Who was that? He snapped off a couple of other shots, while the person, alone, walked farther away. Dressed in jeans and a jean jacket, by the shape, he could tell it was a woman.

Jenae?

TAVIS PULLED UP alongside Deedee's vehicle. Deedee wound down the window, and both she and Shayla looked out at him.

"Shayla, are you heading back to your place?" Tavis asked.

"Yeah," Shayla told him.

"I'll be there soon. I have to check something out."

His gaze wandered ahead, and Shayla tried to follow his line of sight. The crowd was scattering, and she couldn't see whom he was specifically eyeing.

"No problem," she said. "See you soon."

Tavis drove off, and Deedee started up the car and began to move. She drove carefully, as some people were walking into the street to get to their own vehicles.

"Is that how it always is?" Shayla asked. "The balloons, candles, the speeches."

"Yeah," Deedee said. "It's a time for everyone to reflect and remember, and many people want to speak."

Shayla nodded, once again feeling a wave of emotion at the thought of Hayley being cut down in the prime of her life. She wished that she could have spoken up about her friendship with Hayley and how much she'd loved her, but she couldn't dare. Not when she was public enemy number one.

"At least I don't think anyone really noticed us," Deedee said. "That's what I was worried about, and that people would give you a hard time. Like they did at the first vigil."

"I wasn't going to let anyone force me away this time. I needed to be there. It felt… In a way, it felt like a bit of closure. Not fully, but at least I was able to feel close to Hayley without anyone getting in my way."

"I'm glad you got out of it what you wanted."

Shayla had gotten some of what she'd wanted, but not all. "If you don't mind, I'd like to go to the cemetery."

"Why?" Deedee asked.

"I have something… I want to leave it at the grave.

I think it will give me the full closure that I'm looking for."

Deedee's eyes narrowed as she looked at her. "What do you have?"

Shayla wiggled the fingers on her left hand. "The silver band on my pinkie. Hayley gave it to me when we were ten. It's cheap—she won it in a gumball machine. But to me it meant the world, because she said it was proof that we would be BFFs forever. She had one too…" Shayla's voice trailed off. "Anyway, I want to leave it at the grave for her."

Deedee reached for her hand and squeezed. "Oh, hon. I'm so sorry."

"I hope that as she was dying, she knew that I loved her with all my heart. She was the sister I never had."

"I'm sure she did," Deedee said.

"I haven't been able to visit her grave in all these years," Shayla went on. "I feel as though there's unfinished business between us. Words left unsaid. So I want to say them to her. And I hope that wherever she is, she can hear me."

"I totally understand," Deedee said. "Absolutely, I'll take you to the cemetery."

TAVIS SLAMMED A hand against the steering wheel when he realized that he'd lost the mystery woman. With the crowd of people spilling onto the street, he hadn't been able to speed up and follow her. She'd cut sharply around the building, heading toward the back of the school, and he'd pulled up his vehicle several seconds after seeing her head that way, trying to get a better look. His options were either to watch the direction where she was heading and hope that he could drive in that direction and cut her off around the block, or get out of his vehicle and start to follow her.

But the woman, already dodging through the thicket of trees, suddenly started to run.

Tavis pulled the lever to open his door. Then cursed under his breath when he opened it and saw Sheriff Thompson standing there.

"Tavis," he said.

Tavis wanted nothing more than to speed around the block to see if he could catch up with the mystery woman. But Sheriff Thompson was putting a wrench in that plan.

"Sheriff," Tavis said, his voice strained.

"It was a nice vigil today, wasn't it? I didn't see you out there, though."

"I decided to watch from the comfort of my truck."

The sheriff looked beyond him, his gaze landing on the camera with the giant zoom lens. "Doing some sort of surveillance?"

"I always have my gear in my pickup."

"You need all that to provide protection for Shayla Phillips—or is there something else going on?"

"I took pictures of the event. That's not a crime, is it?"

"With that lens? Hmm." The man made it sound like an accusation.

"Yep."

"At least there weren't any problems today. Everything went smoothly."

"Yes, it did." Tavis glanced toward the trees. There was no sign of the woman. "If you—"

"I'm not sure who's been giving her trouble, but I already spoke to Shayla and told her if there are any more threats, she should come to me directly. I'm the one who can help her." He paused. "There haven't been any more threats, have there?"

"Nope," Tavis said, not quite meeting the sheriff's gaze.

"That's good. Then maybe what was written on her car was just someone being a pain in her butt. I doubt anyone's going to do her any harm."

"From your lips to God's ears." Tavis smiled tightly. "But either way, I'm here if there's a real threat or no threat at all."

"I expected you to say that." The sheriff tapped the inside of the Sierra's open window frame. "You have a good day, Tavis."

"You too, sheriff."

DEEDEE WAS DRIVING along Route 1 on the outskirts of town, heading toward the cemetery. She threw a furtive glance into the rearview mirror then said, "Is that guy following me?"

Shayla turned in her seat. There was a large SUV bearing down on them at a rate of speed that was way too fast compared to Deedee's. Route 1 had only one lane in each direction, and when the vehicle on their tail didn't pass them, Deedee sped up.

The SUV accelerated too.

"What's he doing?" Shayla asked, her heart thundering in her chest. Was this just some reckless person on the road? Or someone deliberately following them? She didn't know that anyone had seen them at the vigil, but perhaps someone had. Someone angry enough to—

They both screamed, their bodies jerking forward against their seat belts as the SUV rammed into their car.

"Oh my God!" Deedee exclaimed. She pressed her foot to the gas pedal, speeding up.

"Maybe you should pull over. Let this guy pass you."

"Pull over where? There's no shoulder here. Just gravel, and my car—"

Another jerk, and they screamed again. Clearly, this was no accident. The person behind them *wanted* to do them harm.

Deedee's car fishtailed and she fought to control the steering wheel.

"There," Shayla said, pointing to the county road coming up. "Turn left!"

Deedee hit the gas then slowed a little, anticipating the turn. As she started to turn left, the sound of the SUV's engine revving was all Shayla could register, and her heart caught in her chest.

The SUV slammed into their side. And then the car was spinning wildly. Shayla gripped the armrest on the inside of the door and held on, barely breathing. Gravel exploded in a cloud of smoke as Deedee's car hit the ditch. It spun one final time and then came to a rest on the driver's side. The airbags deployed, hitting Shayla in the face.

For one long moment, there was only silence.

Then Shayla closed her eyes and screamed.

Chapter Ten

Her pulse racing out of control, Shayla couldn't stop screaming. She was dangling in the car, her body leaning left against the seat belt as the Hyundai Sonata was on its side.

Suddenly it hit her. She was the only one screaming. Deedee was silent.

A cold chill sliding down her spine, Shayla was instantly afraid to open her eyes. It seemed like several minutes passed before she dared to do just that, afraid of what she might see.

"Deedee?" she asked, opening her eyes. Her head pounded, making it clear that she hadn't been in some bizarre dream where she'd been stuck on some strange ride at an amusement park, spinning around and around. She was in Deedee's car.

"Deedee…" Shayla's voice croaked as she looked to her left. Deedee sat there motionless, her eyes closed.

Terror seized every part of her body. "Deedee," she repeated, speaking louder this time. "Deedee!"

Deedee said nothing.

The airbag had deployed, and was pressed against

Deedee's face. Surely, the airbag had saved her. So why wasn't she moving?

Oh God. No…

Shayla looked to the rearview mirror, remembering the SUV. But it wasn't there. It was just her and Deedee at the corner of this deserted road en route to the cemetery.

Shayla shook Deedee's shoulder. "Deedee, wake up!"

Blood gushed from Deedee's head, and her eyes remained closed.

Shayla had to get out of the car. She needed to get help. She opened the door, which immediately closed as the weight of gravity pulled it down. Shayla then hit the lever to lower the window and, thankfully, it worked. She undid her seat belt, forced herself past the side and front airbags, and squeezed through the window. She crawled onto the side of the car then hopped down.

As her feet hit solid ground and she drew in a deep breath of fresh air, the reality of the situation hit her. Someone had just tried to kill them. Deedee was unresponsive in the car. She needed to get help.

Shayla's cell phone was in her over-the-shoulder bag, and she quickly accessed it. She punched in Tavis's number.

TAVIS LOOKED AT his phone, saw Shayla's number flashing on his screen. He swiped to answer the call. "Hey—" He stopped short when he heard screaming on the other end of the line. "Shayla?"

"I don't know if Deedee's dead!" came her anguished voice.

Terror gripped Tavis's heart. "Where are you? What happened?"

"Someone ran us off the road!"

"Where?" Tavis demanded.

"Um, I don't know. I...I can't think."

"You said you were heading home. Are you at an intersection?"

"We were heading to the cemetery."

"St. Joseph's Cemetery?"

"Yes."

"So you're somewhere along Route 1."

"Yes. Wait, we're at the corner of County Road 5."

"Okay, I know exactly where you are. I'm on my way."

"Deedee's not moving. She's bleeding." Shayla sobbed. "I'm scared."

"I'm heading to you now. Call 9-1-1."

Tavis ended the call. The sound of terror in Shayla's voice had his gut clenching.

He put his pickup into Drive and tore off.

TAVIS SPED ALONG Route 1, not caring that he was going well over the speed limit. He had to get to Shayla and Deedee.

If someone had purposely run them off the road, then Shayla could still be in danger. And Deedee... He didn't want to believe that she was dead.

Behind him, he heard the sounds of the sirens before he saw the flashing lights in his rearview mirror. Tavis slowed for the cruiser, prepared to pull over, but the cruiser sped around him and continued on. The deputy was heading to the accident scene, no doubt.

By the time Tavis got there, the cruiser was parked on the road and he could see Shayla standing in the ditch beside the silver Hyundai. The car's rear was smashed up pretty badly, and it was on its side. The driver's side.

"Damn," Tavis uttered.

As his gaze wandered, his shock intensified. Rosita and Andrew were on the scene. At first, Tavis's brain didn't compute what he was seeing. Lucas's aunt and uncle? What the heck were they doing there?

Tavis pulled his Sierra to a screeching stop several feet from the accident, then jumped out of his vehicle and trotted back toward Shayla. Moments later, the sheriff's car came whizzing onto the scene.

Seeing him, Shayla hurried to him, and he noticed that she was limping. She threw herself into his arms. "Tavis!"

"I've got you," he said. He held her quivering body against his. He glanced at the wrecked vehicle. "Deedee?"

"She's alive," Shayla said. "But I couldn't get her out."

"We should wait for the firefighters to move her in case she has some internal injuries," Tavis said.

More sirens, then a fire truck was arriving, followed by the paramedics. All emergency personnel were responding to this single vehicle crash.

"You said someone ran you off the road?" Tavis asked. "Are you sure?"

"Someone deliberately hit us. Look at the rear. Then he rammed us from the side and we spun out, landing in the ditch."

Tavis released Shayla and went to further inspect the Hyundai's rear bumper. It was dented and scraped from an impact. "Did you get any information?" he asked. "License plate, make and model?"

"It was a dark car. An SUV. Either navy or black. I couldn't see anything else. I couldn't see who was behind the wheel. But they were definitely after us. After *me*..."

Tavis's gaze wandered to Rosita and Andrew as the sheriff and a paramedic made their way toward Shayla. What were those two doing there? Lucas's aunt and uncle conveniently on the scene?

Tavis didn't like coincidences.

He had seen them drive by the vigil, though they hadn't gotten out of their vehicle. Had they been angry? Angry enough to hurt Shayla? Though their vehicle was black, it wasn't an SUV. And more importantly, there was no damage to it. It couldn't have been the vehicle that forced them off the road.

He stepped toward them, wondering how they had come to be here at this moment. Several feet away, he saw Shayla shaking her head and backing away from the paramedic. "My cousin's the one who needs help," she said.

Tavis turned back to the Carrs. "Rosita and Andrew, hello."

"Hello," Andrew said, slipping an arm around his wife's waist. Her distress was palpable on her face.

"How did you end up at the scene?" Tavis asked, getting to the point.

"We were coming from the cemetery," Andrew answered. "Saw the car in the ditch. Heard the screaming. We pulled over."

It was a reasonable enough explanation. But Tavis pressed on. "You're coming from the cemetery?"

"As you know, today was the vigil for Hayley and Jonathan. We never like to go, but we did drive by today. Then we went to the cemetery to pay our respects. No one wants us at the vigil, but we still feel it's important to honor the victims. Not because we think Lucas killed them," Andrew quickly added. "But because that day changed all of our lives. Two children died who didn't deserve to."

The sheriff wandered over to them. "Andrew and Rosita, Shayla tells me you came upon the scene shortly after the accident."

"Yes," Andrew said.

"You know that Andrew is a retired firefighter," Rosita said. "He could never drive by without stopping to help."

"So you didn't witness the accident as it happened?" Sheriff Thompson asked. "You didn't see who ran them off the road?"

Tavis made his way back over to Shayla while the sheriff spoke to the Carrs. She was hugging her torso as she watched the firefighters in the front and back seats, working on freeing Deedee.

"This is my fault," Shayla said softly. "Someone wanted to kill me, and Deedee is the one paying the price. Maybe if I'd told her about what happened in Buffalo, she would have convinced me not to go today. And she wouldn't be…" Her voice ended on a sob.

"We don't know that this is connected to what happened in Buffalo," Tavis said, though he didn't believe his own words. He kept thinking about the woman in the crowd. Jenae?

"Isn't it?" Shayla asked. "First Buffalo, now this, and you think it's coincidence?"

The question was rhetorical, so Tavis didn't answer. But he didn't like coincidence. However, given Shayla's state of distress, he didn't want to tell her that he may have seen Jenae in the crowd.

"I'm the one they're after," Shayla went on. "They must have seen us at the vigil, then followed us."

"You're saying *they*," Tavis said. "Did you get a look at who was in the vehicle? And was it more than one person?"

Shayla's lips parted, but then her eyes narrowed. "I…I don't know. I couldn't see into the vehicle. All I know is that someone in a navy or black SUV ran us off the road."

Tavis would do his best to find everyone in the town who drove a vehicle that matched that description. But there were a number of them in town, including his.

When Deedee's body emerged on a wooden stretcher, Shayla doubled over with relief. "Oh thank God."

The other firefighters surrounding the car hurried to help carry Deedee to safety. At first, Tavis thought she was unconscious, until he heard her moan softly.

"She's going to be okay," Tavis told Shayla, reassured that she was conscious.

Shayla followed the firefighters to the ambulance, while keeping a respectful distance behind them. As two paramedics helped guide Deedee into the back of their vehicle, the paramedic who'd offered Shayla help returned. "We're going to get your cousin to the hospital as soon as possible. Let me check your vitals, check you for injuries."

"I'm fine," Shayla insisted.

"You could have internal injuries. You really need to go to the hospital to be evaluated."

Tavis placed a hand on the small of Shayla's back. "He's right. You should go."

The car made a loud thud sound as it was finally pulled upright. Seeing the mangled driver's-side door made Tavis realize how serious the attack had been. The Hyundai was far more damaged than he'd realized. That meant Deedee and Shayla had been very very lucky.

"I'll take her," Tavis told the paramedic. "I'll follow the ambulance to the hospital."

When Shayla looked up at him, he said, "We're going there for Deedee, anyway. May as well get you looked at. This is nonnegotiable, Shayla. If you have internal injuries that go undiagnosed, I'll never forgive myself."

Her chest rising with a heavy breath, Shayla nodded. "Okay."

She leaned against him, and he wrapped an arm around her. Every time she turned to him for support, he felt an odd stirring in his gut. He wanted to hold her until all the danger had passed.

"I'm worried about my mother," she said softly. "What if I put her in danger too?"

She pressed her face against his chest and, Lord help him, he wanted to stand there with her like that until she was no longer afraid. "I don't think anyone would hurt your mother. But we now know that this threat is not idle. It's very real. I'm going to have twenty-four-hour surveillance at your place at the back and the front. No one is going to get into your house to hurt you or your mother."

"But no one's there now."

"I'll call one of my guys as soon as we get in the vehicle. Your mother is going to be safe, Shayla. And so are you."

Looking up at him, Shayla nodded, and he could see the gratitude in her eyes. "I appreciate this so much. I promise I'll pay you."

"The only payment I want is you staying safe." Then he gathered her in his arms and held her, feeling a sense of satisfaction as her body melted against his.

And maybe something else he didn't want to acknowledge.

AT FIRST, Shayla had been so pumped up on adrenaline that she hadn't felt any pain and didn't think that she needed medical attention. But once they got to the hospital, she felt the pain in her lower back, her ankle and her head.

Thankfully, she had no broken bones, just some

muscle aches and bruises. She would be fine—but would her cousin?

Now, as she and Tavis waited for word on her cousin's condition, Shayla had made the call to Aunt Maggie and Uncle Charles in North Carolina. They were making immediate plans to return home.

Dr. Nelson, who'd spoken to both Shayla and Tavis earlier about Deedee's condition, entered the waiting room. Tavis shot to his feet. Shayla sat, afraid of what he might say.

"I know I told you that I was worried about brain swelling and the possible complications of that, but we've run extensive tests on Deedee and, long story short, she's very lucky *and* a fighter. The airbag undoubtedly saved her life and protected her skull. She's got a mild concussion and some contusions, and she may suffer some short-term memory loss, but all indications right now are that she's going to be just fine."

"Oh thank God," Shayla uttered.

"That's the best possible news," Tavis said.

"She'll need to stay here for a couple of days for observation, just to make sure there are no unforeseen complications. And of course, she'll need pain management as well. I suspect that will be her biggest challenge." Dr. Nelson paused. "Someone was looking out for you both today."

"How soon can we see her?" Shayla asked.

"She's sleeping right now, but I would say probably in the next hour or so."

As the doctor walked away, Shayla threw her arms around Tavis. "I'm so relieved."

"I know you are. So am I."

"Since we can't see Deedee yet, I'd like to go home and check on my mom. I didn't expect to be gone this long, and I just want to make sure she's all right."

"Absolutely," Tavis agreed.

THE AFTERNOON HAD been a blur of activity, with Shayla's adrenaline racing at warp speed. But now, as Tavis pulled up in front of her mother's place, Shayla realized that her pulse was returning to a somewhat normal pace.

Being with Tavis had made all the difference. He'd been a calming force amid the chaos.

"Thank you so much for being there today," Shayla said. "I'm not sure I could have gotten through this without you."

"There was nowhere else I wanted to be."

Offering him a small smile, Shayla extended her hand and placed it on his. She held his gaze longer than she'd expected, unsurprised by the flash of heat she felt. Quickly, she glanced away.

How silly was she, once again crushing on Tavis? But every time he'd held her today, Shayla had felt as though there was something more between them. She'd wanted to melt into his strong arms and stay there. For a moment, she'd wondered if he'd felt the same way, but Shayla was fairly certain that the feeling was one-sided.

The one thing she did believe, and it made her very happy, was that Tavis didn't hate her anymore.

"We're going to find out who did this to you and

Deedee," Tavis said with steely resolve. "And they're going to pay."

The determination with which he spoke had Shayla believing him. "I know," she said.

"Did you find it odd that Andrew and Rosita were at the accident scene?"

Shayla shook her head. "No, why?"

Tavis's eyebrows rose as he regarded her. "I don't think they're your number one fans."

"True," Shayla said. Rosita and Andrew felt she should have done more to clear Lucas's name. "But they weren't the ones who ran us off the road. You said they told you they were coming from the cemetery. I believe them. I was going to the cemetery for the same reason—to pay my respects away from the prying eyes of the townsfolk."

"I guess I'm grasping at straws here," Tavis said, his lips twisting in a scowl. "It just seems a bit coincidental that they showed up on the scene after the accident—and I don't like coincidences."

"It wasn't them. Nothing about that makes sense."

"There's something else," Tavis said. The silence that followed was heavy. "I didn't want to say this, because I didn't want to upset you. But there was a woman at the vigil today. I didn't get a good look at her, but I was wondering if maybe it was Jenae. If so, that could be the connection here. First, what happened in Buffalo, now this attempt on your life today."

As Shayla digested the words, her lips pulled into a taut line. She couldn't understand this at all. Why would Jenae want to hurt her?

"I can't be certain," Tavis went on. "It's speculation for now. But I couldn't help wondering."

"I saw Alex at the vigil and we spoke for a minute. I asked him if he's in touch with Jenae. His mood changed when I asked about her. He seemed irritated. But he said that they don't talk and he has no idea how to reach her."

"I was going to try to ask him exactly that. You believe him?"

"Oh yeah. Whatever the situation between them, there's no love lost."

Tavis frowned. "Hmm."

"Let's let this go for today. We can rack our brains until they're fried, but hopefully by tomorrow there'll be a clue based on evidence and not speculation. Sheriff Thompson might find the vehicle by then."

"Let's hope," Tavis said, but he didn't sound convinced.

Chapter Eleven

"You gave me quite the scare," Shayla said, unable to contain her smile. She was at Deedee's bedside and holding her hand, her heart brimming with happiness. All things considered, her cousin was okay. A few bruises and bandages weren't reflective of the serious crash she'd been in just the day before.

"You're not getting rid of me that easily," Deedee said.

"I would never want to get rid of you."

With a bit of effort, Deedee smiled. "I know. You talked to my assistant manager?"

"Of course. Don't worry about the restaurant. It's under control."

"And my parents?"

"Will be back soon." They had come to visit bright and early this morning, not stopping at home after arriving from North Carolina. "Your mother said she was going home to make you some—and I quote—'edible food.'"

Deedee chuckled. "Of course. My mother's probably worried that I'll waste away during the time I spend here."

Shayla grinned then swallowed as a spate of sadness hit her. So many years she'd lived away from her mother, and now her mother might not have much time left.

"I'm so sorry," Shayla said, and her happy tone turned serious. "I never should have insisted that we go to that vigil. If I'd ever known—"

"You wouldn't have gone. I know." Deedee squeezed her hand. "It's not your fault."

"But you didn't want me to go, and I was so determined. Now you're here…"

"Exactly. I'm *here*. A little banged up, but still kicking. And you're still here too."

Shayla nodded. That was the most important thing—that the attempt on their lives had failed.

There was a knock at the door before it opened a smidgen. Deputy Jenkins stuck his head into the room. "Can I come in?"

"Sure," Deedee said.

"I hope you're up to answering some questions this morning. I did get Shayla's statement already, but you might be able to fill in some more blanks."

Deedee began to sit up in the bed, wincing as she did. Shayla slipped her hands beneath Deedee's underarms and helped ease her up.

"I'm ready to tell you what I remember," Deedee said.

Shayla was relieved that the doctor had been wrong. Deedee did seem to have her short-term memory, so that was good. She hadn't suffered any memory loss whatsoever. All things considered, this was a miracle.

Even Shayla's aches and pains and twisted ankle would heal. She only hoped that the person who had done this to them was caught quickly.

The deputy came to stand beside the bed and then dug his notepad out of his jacket. "Tell me what you remember."

"I was driving toward St. Joseph's Cemetery. Then, out of the blue, there was a van behind us." Deedee winced. "A van or an SUV."

"You think it was a van?" Shayla asked.

"Maybe. I mean, I think it was an SUV, but it could've been a van, maybe. Or one of those pickup trucks on steroids. You know, those big, shiny ones."

"I suppose it could have been a Ford F-150 or one of those monster pickups," Shayla agreed. "Or an SUV. But I don't think it was a van."

"So a pickup truck or an SUV or maybe a van." Deputy Jenkins scrawled some notes.

"And it was black," Deedee added. "I'm pretty sure of that."

"Did you recognize it at all?" the deputy asked. "Have you seen anyone in town with such a vehicle?"

"I'm not sure what vehicle it was, so no, I didn't recognize it per se. But there are a lot of people in town with vehicles that look like that. Chase, for one. He has one of those big pickups, and it's black. But he's not the only one. There are a number of them."

"Chase was at the vigil," Deputy Jenkins said. "I saw him there. And, given the timing when you left, I don't think he could have been the one to run you off the road. He was talking to his father for quite some time after everyone dispersed."

"I didn't say it was him," Deedee pointed out. "You asked if I know anyone with such a vehicle. He's someone I know with a black pickup or an SUV. His brother too. Tavis. Probably thirty per cent of the men in this town."

The deputy scrawled more notes. "And you feel that you were deliberately targeted? This wasn't simply an accident? Maybe kids being stupid?"

"I remember the vehicle speeding up behind me. I started to drive faster, thinking that would appease the driver. But whoever was behind the wheel started to drive even faster. I wanted to pull over onto the gravel to let them pass me, but it was a two-lane road and nothing else was coming in the opposite direction, so I thought the driver would just overtake me. Then the next thing I know, he's hitting my bumper. I thought maybe it was a mistake. Until he hit me again. And then I quickly went to turn, because there was a side road coming up. I started to turn, and that's the last thing I remember..."

Shayla looked at the deputy. "This was deliberate. And I know I was the target. I've already spoken to Sheriff Thompson about some of the threats I've received, and I know this was directed at me. I was really shaken up and distraught yesterday, but today I'm angry. I could've been killed, and my cousin could've been killed. Why? Because people in this town won't let something go that I had nothing to do with. So today, I'm livid. I want this person caught. I want him caught now."

"I understand your frustration," the deputy said. "That's why we have to ask these questions. The more we know, the faster we can bring the culprit to justice."

"This is a small enough town," Shayla went on. "How hard can it be to search a database and find everyone who has a similar vehicle? Then find the person who has either just repainted the vehicle or has it in the shop somewhere."

The deputy gave her a wry smile. "I see you like to watch a lot of crime shows."

Was that meant as an insult? "Some things are common sense," Shayla said. "I'm just hoping that you're on top of this, because what happened yesterday was very serious and could have been deadly. It's a miracle that neither of us was killed."

"I agree." The deputy looked at Deedee again. "Do you have anything else to add? Anything that you think may be important?"

She shook her head. "No. I don't even remember the impact. Maybe that's a good thing. All I remember is at one point waking up and feeling somewhat disoriented and not knowing what was going on. The next thing I knew, I was in this hospital room."

Shayla stroked her cousin's forehead. Once again, she thought of how she could have lost her, and a wave of emotion gripped her heart.

"Please, deputy," Shayla said. "Find whoever did this. And find him quickly."

TAVIS STOOD OUTSIDE the hospital room with Deedee's parents. They had gone home a couple of hours ago and now had returned, Deedee's mother holding a tote bag from which emanated some seriously delicious smells. He had stopped Deedee's parents before they could enter her room, letting them know that the deputy was in with them.

"I hope he won't take too long. I want to make sure my daughter has some good food to eat. Hospital food." She made a face. "It's barely sufficient."

"It didn't take you too long to whip up something that smells amazing," Tavis said.

"Sweet and sour chicken with sticky rice," Maggie said. "I can prepare you a plate if you like. There's enough for two."

A smile tugged at Tavis's lips. He would love nothing more than to indulge in a meal, but he declined. "Deedee's going to need all the food she can get. I know that what they serve at hospitals is paltry and unappetizing. She's lucky she has you."

The door opened and the deputy exited. Maggie and Charles whizzed into the room.

Deputy Jenkins had his cell phone to his ear, and walked a good distance away as he chatted. Tavis couldn't hear what he was saying, but he watched him intently.

Several minutes later, Deputy Jenkins ended the call. Then he headed toward Tavis. "You wanted a word with me?"

"Yes," Tavis said. "Have you been checking local body shops to see if anyone brought in a vehicle for repair?"

"You sound like Shayla."

Tavis didn't ask him to elaborate. "Obviously the vehicle that ran them off the road is going to have some damage. It's going to pop up somewhere."

"I just got some news on that front," the deputy said, indicating the phone in his hand. "Both good and bad."

"Oh?" Tavis's eyebrows shot up.

"The vehicle that ran them off the road has been located."

"Why didn't you say so?" Tavis asked. Finally, there was a break.

"Well, that's where the bad news comes in. The good news is we found the vehicle, but the bad news is, the person it belongs to most certainly isn't the one who ran them off the road."

Tavis's gut began to sink. "You sure about that? You can't rule anyone out."

"The vehicle belongs to Aaron Burke," the deputy said, and let his words sink in. "I'm sure you can agree that Aaron Burke would not be the person behind the wheel of that SUV when Deedee and Shayla were run off the road."

Aaron Burke was one of the town's most high-profile residents. A famous soccer star, Tavis couldn't see it either. He had no connection to the case, though he did know the kids from school.

"Mr. Burke reported his vehicle stolen last night. It was found ditched the next county over."

"Darn it," Tavis uttered. "Hopefully the perp didn't wipe it down."

"He did one better. He torched it."

"Son of a—" Tavis clenched his teeth. Someone was really making sure to conceal their tracks. "Then there were two of them. If the SUV was ditched the next county over, whoever drove it there would need a ride back."

"He could have used a ride-sharing service—which we're checking," Deputy Jenkins added before Tavis could ask the question.

"Hopefully he—or they—made a mistake."

"At first I thought it might've been a couple kids who were stupid, possibly drinking. But the fact that the SUV was torched tells me this was something different."

"It sure as hell was. And it's a miracle that there were no fatalities because of this." Tavis blew out a frustrated breath. "Man, I was hoping we'd catch a break with the SUV. Instead we're back at square one."

"*I'm* back at square one," the deputy clarified. "The sheriff's department is back at square one. You're not."

Tavis said nothing. He had some leeway where Deputy Jenkins was concerned, and he didn't want to push it. No, he wasn't officially investigating this case, but he'd be damned if he wasn't going to do what he could to find out who was behind the attack. Someone had nearly killed Shayla and her cousin—on his watch. He wouldn't soon forgive himself for that. The only way to atone for it was to find out who'd done it.

"Oh," the deputy said. "I almost forgot. You asked me for a favor."

Tavis stood straight, perking up. "Yes. You have an answer?"

The deputy took a couple of steps, moving farther away from the waiting room area and out of earshot. "I found out that Jenae changed her name," the deputy said in a low voice. "Looks like she wanted to escape Alex."

"That's a pretty serious reaction. Was he abusive?"

"There were rumors that he had a bad temper, but I never heard that he hit her. But maybe once they split, she was afraid of him? Now, I'm not saying he would've hurt her, but she must've believed that to change her name. Or maybe she simply wanted a complete break from him. I heard they had a really ugly divorce."

"Yeah, someone mentioned that. About the divorce." Tavis hesitated for a beat then asked, "What's her new name?"

"I don't know. I spoke with her parents, and all they'd tell me was that she'd changed her name."

"You have a way for me to reach her?" Tavis asked.

"Unfortunately, I don't. Because here's the thing. Her parents said they haven't heard from her in over a week. They're worried. They put in a missing persons report in Erie, where she was living and last seen."

"Erie? I heard that she lived in Buffalo."

"At one time I think she did, but her parents said she very recently moved to Erie."

This didn't make sense. At all. "The parents filed a missing persons report? So you're telling me that Jenae Wilkinson is missing?"

"That's what her parents said."

"For more than a week?"

"Apparently."

If Jenae was living in Erie, then what was the connection to the house in Buffalo? And Lucas?

"Thanks," Tavis said. But he was more confused than ever and no closer to any answers.

ALL NIGHT, Tavis tried to put the pieces of the puzzle together, but couldn't. Was Jenae actually missing? Surely her parents wouldn't have filed a missing persons report if she wasn't. That had Tavis wondering about what Deedee had said.

Deedee had told him that she'd contacted someone who'd contacted Jenae only a couple of days ago. But if that were true, then Jenae *wasn't* missing. Or had Deedee been lying?

But why would Deedee lie? Surely she wouldn't do anything to put her cousin, or herself, in jeopardy. And yet, he had gotten the feeling that she hadn't been completely forthright with him.

Tavis dragged a hand over his face. Maybe he was losing his mind, suspecting everyone and everything. It had been a lot of years of searching for Lucas, investigating every angle he could, and hoping for a break. Maybe it was all getting to him.

Regardless, he needed to talk to Deedee again. But with her still in the hospital, he didn't want to push her while she was recovering. He needed more answers, and maybe the best way to get them was to go directly to Jenae's parents.

"Hey, Griffin," he said into the phone. "You okay to stay at Shayla's house for about thirty, forty, minutes?"

"Sure thing."

"There's something I need to do, then I'll head right there to relieve you."

"No problem. I'm good."

"Thanks, Griffin."

Tavis downed a cup of coffee then headed out to the Wilkinson place. He pulled into the driveway of the old Victorian house, noting that there was no car in the driveway. But the vehicles could be parked in the detached garage.

Tavis exited his GMC Sierra, then walked up the steps to the wraparound porch and the front door. It was a beautiful house, painted a bright yellow. A porch swing moved gently with the breeze, and wind chimes sang.

Tavis rang the doorbell. Waited.

Nothing. He rang the bell again, straining to make sure that he could hear it. It was working. But when again there was no response, he knocked. A full minute later, no one had come to the door.

Tavis stepped to the right and peered through the window, hoping that any neighbors seeing him would not think he was up to no good. He could see the outline of a living room and the kitchen at the back through the sheer curtains, but he saw no signs of life.

He turned on his heel and headed down the steps.

"They're not there," came a voice.

He whirled around, seeing an older woman standing on the porch of the neighboring house.

"Oh?" he asked.

"They haven't been there since yesterday, before the vigil. They took off in a real hurry."

"Took off, hmm?"

"I think they're worried about their daughter. They didn't say much. They just packed up their car and left."

"And they were heading to find Jenae? That's what they told you?"

"They didn't really say. I saw them briefly and asked where they were going, and Laura said that they needed to get to Jenae."

"She in some kind of trouble?" Tavis asked, ambling over to the other house.

"I'm not sure. Such a sweet girl. Shame she has to be worried about that fool she married."

"Alex," Tavis supplied.

"I never thought he was any good. He's made her life hell, he has."

"I heard things ended badly."

The woman harrumphed. "He didn't want to let her go. Though only God knows why. It wasn't like he treated her well."

Tavis pulled his phone from his jeans' pocket. "You have a way for me to reach the Wilkinsons?"

The woman suddenly seemed to think better of her rambling mouth, and now eyed Tavis with suspicion. "What's your business with them?"

"I've been trying to find Jenae. I'm…in the personal protection business. I can help."

"Why don't you give me your number and I can pass it on to them. I'm not sure I can reach them, because I've called a couple of times and haven't heard anything. But I'll leave them a message all the same."

Tavis reached into his back pocket for a business card. "That'd be great."

Chapter Twelve

The next morning, Shayla's cell phone rang. Seeing the Sheridan Falls prefix, she answered. "Hello?"

"Shayla, it's Chase from Lucky's Auto."

"Oh yes. Hello."

"Your car's done. Would you like me to come pick you up?"

"No, that's not necessary. I can get a ride there. I can come anytime?"

"I'm here all day," he said, then chuckled.

"Excellent. I'll see you soon."

Shayla let the nurse know that she would be heading out for a short bit. Aunt Maggie was visiting her mother, so thankfully her mom wasn't alone. Aunt Maggie would head to the hospital in the afternoon to pick up Deedee, who was expected to be discharged after some final tests. Shayla would be home well before then.

Shayla went out to Tavis's Sierra. Seeing her coming, he wound down his window.

"Hey," Shayla said. "I got a call that my car is ready. Do you mind driving me to Lucky's Auto Shop?"

"Right now?"

"Yep. My aunt is with my mom, and the nurse is there. I think we're fine to leave for a little while."

Tavis glanced around then started his ignition. "I agree. Hop in."

Within minutes, they were at Lucky's Auto Shop. Chase smiled when she entered, the smile wavering slightly when he saw Tavis enter the shop behind her.

"Shayla, hello. Tavis."

"Hello, Chase."

"Your car is as good as new."

"Where is it?"

"In the back bay. Follow me."

Shayla did just that, and Tavis fell into step beside her. Together, they went into the bay area of the shop where there was one car hoisted up, another with its hood raised, and then her car, looking shiny and new.

"As I explained," Chase began, "I had to repaint the entire right side in order to match the paint and make it look good. I detailed the whole car to make it look brand-new."

Shayla examined the right side of the car, then the rest of the vehicle. The royal blue looked perfect.

"Thanks so much," she said, now inspecting the windshield. There was no indication that it had ever been vandalized. It glistened.

"You were at the vigil a couple of days ago," Tavis said.

Chase wiped his palms against his navy mechanic's jumpsuit. "Yeah, yeah I was."

"I suppose you heard what happened—someone running Shayla and her cousin off the road?"

"Yeah, I heard." He made a sound of derision as he shook his head. "I couldn't believe it. Who would want to hurt them? You might not know, but Deedee and I used to date. Back in high school."

"Yeah, I remember." Tavis looked around at the other cars, and then outside at the cars lined up waiting for work. "You hear anything? Any word about who might have run Shayla and Deedee off the road?"

"No." Chase shook his head. "But no one would tell me that."

"But this is a small town. You must have people coming in and out of here all day. Word gets out."

"I did hear that the vehicle was found, burned. People like that don't tend to brag about what they've done."

Tavis nodded, acknowledging that fact. "Do me a favor, will you? You hear anything, will you let me know?"

Chase looked at him for a long moment. "I'll let my dad know. He's the one investigating this. The sheriff's department."

Shayla watched as the two men stared each other down. There was animosity between them. Or was she imagining it?

"Thank you," she said to Chase in an effort to put an end to the unspoken tension. "I guess I just need to sign the paperwork and collect the keys, then I can leave."

Chase turned his attention to her, offering a big smile. "That's right. We can go back inside, take care of everything."

Chase led the way, and Shayla followed. Tavis lingered for a moment, and when Shayla looked over her shoulder at him, she saw him glancing around the shop.

Was he looking for something? And if so, what?

"WHAT WAS THAT ABOUT?" Shayla asked when she and Tavis were finished and outside.

Tavis shrugged. How could he tell her that all of the Thompson men rubbed him the wrong way? The sheriff was a thorn in his side, and his sons had always been spoiled and entitled.

"A bit of bad blood," Tavis admitted.

"Because of what?"

Tavis's cell phone trilled. He quickly accessed his phone, happy for an excuse to avoid answering Shayla. The problems between him and the Thompsons weren't worth getting into.

When he read the text, his stomach dropped.

"What is it?" Shayla asked, and he could hear the alarm in her voice.

"I just got a text," he explained. "It says, 'Stop looking for me, you're going to get me killed.'"

Shayla's eyes bulged. "What?"

He angled the phone so she could see it for herself.

"Who?" Shayla asked. "Jenae?"

"Maybe," Tavis said. "It's a Buffalo number, and she was living there." He pressed the number on the screen, and it began to dial. He brought the phone to his ear.

"The number you are calling cannot be reached. Please check the number and try again."

Shayla stared at him expectantly.

"The number can't be reached." He frowned. "Probably one of those apps. You can text but you can't call someone back."

"But why would Jenae send you such a message?" Shayla frowned.

"I went to her parents' place. I was hoping to find them and see if I could locate her." At least he knew now that she'd gotten the message. He explained the interaction he'd had with the neighbor and that he'd left her a number to pass along to Jenae's parents so they could reach him.

Tavis sent a reply text, hoping it would go through to the sender.

Who is this? If you need help, I can help you.

"I sent the person a text," he said. "I hope it goes through to whoever it is and they'll respond." Staring at his phone, he made a face. According to Deputy Jenkins, Jenae had been missing for over a week. Her parents were clearly worried, which had him wondering if she'd met with foul play.

Suddenly, it didn't make sense that she was the one who'd sent the text.

"Listen," Tavis began, "I need to talk to your cousin about something. But I won't do it yet. I know she's recovering, and I don't want to upset her. But I got news from Deputy Jenkins. According to him, Jenae's been missing for over a week. That's why her parents left, apparently to try and find her. But Deedee said she spoke to someone who relayed my message to Jenae only a couple of days ago. If her own parents can't reach her, how could a friend?"

"Deedee wouldn't lie. If she said she got word from Jenae, then she did."

"Shayla, I'm told her parents filed a missing persons report."

"You don't think Jenae sent that text?"

"Maybe it was Lucas?" Tavis suggested. "Unless Jenae isn't missing, but she's gone underground. I'm going to do a records search on that house in Buffalo, see who owns it."

"I feel like we're fighting a ghost," Shayla said.

"I wonder if it's possible that Jenae was in the crowd at the vigil."

"You just said she's missing."

"Yeah, but there was a woman at the vigil. I didn't get a good look at her. I took pictures, but with what happened to you and Deedee, I haven't gone through them all yet. Maybe you can come to my place and go through the pictures with me. See if you recognize anyone that I may not. We might even get an idea of who might have followed you and run you off the road."

"Now?" Shayla asked.

"Now's as good a time as any," Tavis said. "We don't have to take too long. Maybe thirty minutes to go through the photos?"

"I guess my mother should be fine in the meantime. The real threat is to me—and if anyone has been watching, then they'll know that I'm with you. Besides, it's the middle of the day. I doubt there'll be any problems right now. I'll just text the nurse to tell her that I'll be back later than I expected."

"Great," Tavis said. "Follow me to my place."

SHAYLA FOLLOWED TAVIS through the main streets of Sheridan Falls until he turned onto a tree-lined street with modern houses, built probably within the last ten to fifteen years. Halfway down the street, he turned right into a double-car driveway and she did the same. As she turned off her car, she looked out at the two-story, redbrick home. It had a moderate-sized lawn that was somewhat parched, but the shrubs surrounding the front porch were a vibrant green.

Shayla exited the vehicle and followed Tavis up the steps to his front door. Her gaze wandered from his home to him, taking in the sight of him from behind, from head to toe. His wide shoulders and muscular back, and those very strong biceps. As far as bodyguards went, she couldn't do better. Tavis made her feel protected and safe.

And he also made her feel something else. Looking at him now, she was suddenly very aware of him as a man. He was strong, sexy and undeniably hot. But she hadn't spoken to him in nearly nine years, and there'd been animosity when they had. So how was it that she still felt any level of attraction for him now?

She turned and gazed out at the quiet street. Two young children were playing on a lawn three houses over, squealing with delight as they jumped through a sprinkler. It made her think for a moment of the life she hadn't considered. A life with a husband

and kids, and being normal. Not a life where she felt shame and fear because of the tragic incident that happened in her life years ago.

"You coming?" Tavis asked.

She spun around at the sound of his voice. "Yes. Of course."

She followed him into the house, and instantly took note of the cream-colored walls, which were mostly bare except for a couple of black-and-white photos of city skylines. To the right was the living room, with a large black leather sectional and a giant flat-screen television. The pictures in the living room were of abstract art. There was nothing in particular that made this place his. No pictures of him or his family.

It was the quintessential bachelor pad.

"I have everything upstairs," he told her.

Shayla followed him to the second level. She blew out a haggard breath. The idea of going upstairs with him had her thinking of something else entirely—which made no sense. It wasn't as if Tavis had invited her here for a romantic date.

When he opened the door to a bedroom, all misplaced thoughts of attraction fled her mind. She immediately saw the wall with pictures of Hayley and Jonathan and her and Deedee and Alex and…pretty much everyone they'd gone to school with. Everyone who'd been at the party anyway. He had an entire wall with tons of pictures and notes and arrows pointing between people.

She stepped into the room. "What is this?"

"Everything I've come up with regarding the murders. Everyone who was at the party, everyone who had a story to tell me about what they believed happened."

She looked up at him. "I wasn't at the party."

"No, but you were connected to Lucas." He pointed, showing her how the line from Lucas led to her and the words written there. *Does she know where Lucas is? Did he tell her what he was going to do?*

"You know now that I don't know where he is. You know that he never told me what he was up to."

He used his fingers to wipe away what he'd written between the line connecting her and Lucas. "I haven't updated it."

Shayla looked at the board, folding her arms over her chest as she inspected all the work he had done. "Wow. This is everyone."

She frowned when she realized he had written something else, which must have been recent.

Rosita and Andrew? At the scene coincidentally?

She whipped around to face him. "Didn't you tell me that you don't think they had anything to do with the accident?"

"I don't believe that they do, no. But…I like to put everything down just to be sure. Sometimes it sparks another question, and I can go back to something and see things differently."

"You put a lot of work into this."

"And that's not all." He walked toward one of his filing cabinets, opened it and withdrew a binder. "In here, I have interviews with everyone. I transcribed them all."

She wandered over to him, saw the amount of pages and gasped softly. "Tavis…"

And it struck her then just how determined he was. But his cousin had been killed. Of course he was determined.

She looked at him. "I didn't even imagine how much this has been eating at you. I…"

She reached for his arm, gently laid her hand on it. He looked at her, holding her gaze for a long beat. Shayla had the overwhelming urge to put her arms around him and offer him the kind of comfort he had offered her yesterday.

Before she could, he stepped away. He moved to the desk where his laptop was and opened it. "I uploaded all of the photos from the memory card. You want to go through them now?"

Shayla went to stand beside him. Her heart was beating faster than normal. "Sure."

The first picture was of the crowd at large, with the grieving families up front on the school steps. Tavis rose and grabbed another chair so she could sit. When she did, he continued clicking through the photos.

Chase and his wife. Alex. Her and Deedee. Many of the people she'd seen in the crowd. Most of them familiar faces. No one in town she specifically knew would want to hurt her, except Jonathan's grandfather, who'd pulled a gun on her, and maybe Tammy, who'd thrown water in her face.

"These are all the townsfolk," she said. "Everybody I know."

Tavis continued going through the photos. "What about her?"

Shayla squinted to see, but the photo had been taken from a far distance. "It's a bit fuzzy. I can't fully see her."

He zoomed it in. "Today, I was wondering if that might be Jenae with an altered appearance, though I don't know. She looks different. But something about her got my attention." He went to the next picture, a closer version of the woman.

And Shayla's mouth fell open as she realized who the woman in the baseball hat was.

"Oh my God."

"You know her."

"That's my mother's nurse." She looked at Tavis, who met her with a questioning gaze. "The day of the vigil, she called in sick. She told me she had the flu and she couldn't make it in to take care of my mother."

"You're sure?" Tavis asked.

"Yes! That's her!" She pointed at the screen, stopping short of jabbing it. "But she wasn't sick, obviously. Which means she lied to me."

"I thought she had dark hair."

"She's definitely not blond, so that must be a wig," Shayla said. "Unless she dyed her hair."

"I've never seen her in this town before. Have you?"

"No. Never. I only met her when I came back here. So if she's not even from Sheridan Falls, what the heck was she doing at the vigil?"

Chapter Thirteen

Shayla raced back to her house. Suddenly, she was terrified for the safety of her mother. Even though she had left her there with her aunt and the replacement nurse, knowing that Jennifer had been at the vigil and had lied had her feeling a sense of betrayal she couldn't quite explain. Was the home care nurse's whole appearance in Sheridan Falls based on false pretenses? Had she taken the job in an effort to get close to her?

Shayla rushed into the house, immediately greeting Melanie, the replacement nurse. The woman looked at her with concern. "Is everything okay?" she asked.

"Jennifer. The other nurse who has been here. Do you know her?"

"No. The agency called me to replace her. Why?"

"Have you ever met her?"

The door opened and Tavis entered. The nurse looked between Shayla and Tavis, a sense of growing unease obvious on her face. "What's this about?"

"I have reason to believe that she is not who she

said she is. And she's been in this house with my mother."

"I…I don't know what to tell you."

"How did you hire her?" Tavis asked Shayla. "Through an agency?"

"Yes. An agency out of Buffalo. I had no reason to be concerned." She looked to Melanie again. "My aunt left?"

"About twenty minutes ago. She said she needed to get to the hospital."

Shayla rushed down the hallway to the den. Seeing her mother sleeping, a relieved breath eased out of her. She didn't know what was going on, but she didn't like it.

"If the other nurse has done something, I suggest you call the agency to report her. Or I can, if you'd like."

"No," Shayla said forcefully. "Do not call the agency." She took a deep breath. She didn't want this woman to be alarmed enough to call the agency, because maybe Jennifer would never show her face again. And she needed Jennifer to show her face again to get answers.

"There's no need," Shayla went on. "I…I just need to clarify something. Maybe I've misconstrued the situation. Understandably, I'm very protective of my mother."

"Of course," Melanie said. "I can tell you that your mother has been taken care of very well. From the notes I've seen, nothing is out of order. But you can ask Jennifer tomorrow. I've already gotten word from the agency that she'll be back."

Shayla threw a glance over her shoulder at Tavis.

"Tomorrow." She smiled. "Perfect. I'll talk to her then."

TOMORROW COULDN'T COME fast enough as far as Shayla was concerned. Thankfully, the evening provided distractions from her obsessing over the situation with Jennifer. Deedee had been released from the hospital and Shayla, along with her aunt and uncle, had helped get her settled at home. Afterward, she went back home to her mother, tipped Melanie generously for agreeing to stay a couple more hours, then when Melanie was gone, curled up beside her mother and played a movie for them to watch.

Tavis hadn't wanted to leave, not with the word about Jennifer. So he hadn't had Griffin relieve him. Instead, Tavis was planning to stay outside Shayla's place the entire night.

He was going above and beyond, and she definitely appreciated him for that.

At about one in the morning, Shayla couldn't sleep. Tavis was out in his vehicle, keeping watch over her house, and that didn't sit right with Shayla. The least she could do was offer him a comfortable sofa.

Shayla slipped into a robe then went outside. Crickets chirped, the only sound at this hour. She made her way to Tavis's pickup. She heard the locks click open before she could knock on the passenger's-side window.

Shayla opened the door. "Why don't you come inside? I hate the idea of you being stuck in your truck all night."

"I'm fine here."

Shayla glanced around. The street was quiet, and seemed safe. "I'd prefer you come inside. I…I'll feel better. Safer."

"Are you sure?"

"Let me get you something to eat, something to drink. You can still do your job, but from inside my house. Arguably, it could be better for you to be inside. What if someone tries to access the house from the back? I know you're the only one here tonight."

"All right," Tavis agreed.

Shayla walked back into the house, leaving him to gather his belongings. She stepped into the kitchen and started the kettle.

When she heard Tavis enter, she went to the foyer to meet him. In a quiet voice, she said, "I started the kettle. Would you like some tea? Or if you like coffee, I can make that."

"I'm fine with tea. Two sugars."

"Now what about something to eat? There's some fried chicken in the fridge as well. Can I get you a plate?"

Tavis hesitated then nodded. "I'd love a plate."

Shayla felt good as she set about preparing some food for him. He was giving her so much, she wanted to do something nice for him.

She set the plate and the tea on the kitchen table for him.

"This smells amazing, thank you," he said.

"Feel free to set your laptop up here," Shayla said.

Tavis dug in, moaning happily as he ate a piece of the chicken. "This is delicious."

"I'm glad you like it. The least I can do is give you a decent meal."

Tavis sipped some tea. "I think it's a good idea if I set up a couple of cameras in the backyard—until the person who wants to hurt you is caught. I'll always be out front, or one of my guys, but setting up a camera or two at the front is probably a smart idea too."

"Tell me what I need to get. I'll go buy it."

He nodded, unable to speak as he ate some of the mac and cheese.

"You know," she went on, "I was thinking about something. You asked me if I knew what Lucas was up to—and I didn't, of course. People seem to keep asking me about him and if I'd known about his criminal enterprise—which I didn't. But when I think back to that day, he had seemed a bit anxious. I'm not sure why. But he'd even asked me the day before if I would consider leaving town with him."

Tavis lowered the piece of chicken he'd been about to bite. "He asked you to leave town? You knew he was planning to leave?"

"I didn't know that he was going to leave for sure, just that he asked if I would go with him. I told him that I couldn't do that. For one, we'd only been dating for like a month or so. I found the request bizarre. But the big thing I'm remembering now is that he seemed on edge, uneasy about something. I don't know why I didn't consider that before. I don't know if it has anything to do with why he left, or why he did what he did. And he didn't tell me what was bothering him. Maybe nothing was, and I'm reading too much into the memory. Or maybe he knew

he was planning to leave and he didn't want our relationship to end?"

Tavis pursed his lips. "I don't know what to make
of that."

"Neither do I. But I thought I'd tell you. I don't
know… Maybe it's nothing."

Shayla left Tavis to eat and returned to the counter,
where she decided to use the time to unload the dishwasher. Once it was cleared, she put the few dishes
from the sink into the dishwasher.

"Where's your green bin?"

Shayla whipped around, throwing a hand over her
heart. Somehow, Tavis had appeared right beside her
and she hadn't even heard him.

"Under the sink," she told him. "Right here."

She opened the cupboard, took the plate from him
and scraped the bones into the green bin. Then she
put the plate and utensils into the dishwasher.

"Where's your bathroom?"

"Down the hall, first door on the left."

Tavis disappeared, and Shayla made sure that
everything was put away in the kitchen. Then she
wandered down the hallway and checked in on her
mother. She was sleeping. When she turned around,
she met Tavis as he was walking away from the bathroom.

"Do you want a pillow, a blanket? I can get that
for you if you think you might want to take a little
nap on the sofa. You've been here all day."

"I don't want to sleep on the job," he told her.

"Let me get you a pillow and a blanket anyway. I
feel…I feel safe with you here regardless."

She quickly went upstairs to the linen closet and got a comforter and a pillow. She returned downstairs with the items, placing them on the sofa. "And if there's anything else you need, just let me know."

The lamps were off in the living room, but the light from the kitchen provided soft illumination. Shayla looked up at Tavis, and he looked down at her. "I really do appreciate you being here for me," she said, her voice soft. "For everything you've done."

And then she was stepping toward him and placing a hand on his chest. She held his gaze, wondering what had come over her. They'd been through so much over the last few days, and Shayla felt a growing connection to him. The idea of heading back to Miami and not seeing him again was a thought she'd already had, and she didn't like it. It was silly, she knew, but there was something about him that excited her. Years ago, and now.

Her chest rose and fell with an anxious breath as she waited for him to reject her, to put a stop to her crazy fantasy. Instead, he slowly ran his fingers up her arm and then across her shoulder blade.

His touch set her skin on fire. And the look in his eyes told her that her attraction wasn't one-sided. Slowly, he leaned toward her. Shayla tipped up on her toes. Their lips met tentatively, and then he slipped both arms around her, held her close and deepened the kiss.

Everything inside Shayla's body came alive as his hands roamed her back and his tongue swept over hers. She looped her arms around his neck and held on.

"Maybe we shouldn't," he said on a raspy breath.

"Why not?" she asked. "I'm a big girl. I want this."

And she did. She wanted one night with her old crush. One night where she got to fully feel what it was like to have a man like him love her.

She took him by the hand and led him upstairs. She giggled slightly, imagining having done this as a teen—sneaking a boy up to her room. She hadn't done it as a teenager, but now was doing it as a twenty-seven-year-old.

She led him into her bedroom, closed the door and then took her robe off. Tavis slipped his hands beneath her nightshirt, and when his fingers moved over her breasts, she moaned. His touch felt like heaven.

She pulled her nightshirt off and tossed it aside, while Tavis removed his gun and holster and then his shirt. Moonlight and streetlight filtered through the blinds, and Shayla took a moment to admire his muscular chest. What a specimen of a man!

He moved toward her and kissed her cheek softly. Then the other cheek. And then he began to softly kiss her lips. She melted against him, surrendering to this man who had always excited her.

"I probably shouldn't be doing this," he said. "But I don't want to stop."

"I don't want to stop, either." One night with her crush...

Tavis led her to the bed, where they kissed and worked at getting out of the remainder of their clothes. Then Tavis pulled her into his arms, and Shayla gave herself up completely to the sweet heat consuming them.

MAKING LOVE WITH Tavis had been incredible, and provided Shayla some time where she wasn't obsessing over Jennifer. He lay with her in bed for half an hour afterward, making Shayla feel as though the sex hadn't simply been sex. Though he had only just returned downstairs to resume his protection duties, she missed him.

Not that they were about to sail off into the sunset. The sex had been something they'd both wanted, and perhaps needed, given all the stress of the recent days.

And the morning was going to bring more stress once she confronted Jennifer.

When Shayla got up bright and early and went downstairs, Tavis wasn't in the house. He'd packed up his laptop too. Shayla looked out the front window. His vehicle was there.

He'd returned to his Sierra.

Maybe he hadn't wanted to be inside the house when the nurse came? Or maybe he'd considered that he might startle her mother if she got up in the night?

Shayla checked on her mother, found her sleeping. Thankfully. Hopefully, she continued to sleep when Jennifer arrived so she wouldn't overhear any of the conversation. To be on the safe side, Shayla closed the door to the den.

Ten minutes later, as Shayla was drinking a cup of coffee at the kitchen table, she heard the nurse enter the house. Nerves fluttering in her stomach, she got up and headed to the foyer.

Seeing her, Jennifer greeted her with a bright smile. Gone was the blond hair, meaning she'd been wearing a wig at the vigil. "Good morning, Shayla. How are you today?"

"I'm great," Shayla said. "You're feeling better?"

"Yeah, nothing that a couple of days of rest couldn't cure."

"You look good. The rest agreed with you."

There was a knock at the door. It had to be Tavis.

"Let me go check on your mother," Jennifer said.

"Definitely. I'll get the door."

Jennifer ambled off down the hallway, and Shayla headed to the front door. As she opened it, she realized that her heart was beating fast. Tavis looked down at her, and she nodded. "Let's do this."

Tavis entered the home, and she guided him into the living room. She didn't want to confront the nurse while she was with her mother. A few minutes later, Jennifer was walking into the living room, her eyes widening when she saw Tavis.

"You remember Tavis," Shayla said.

"Yes." Jennifer smiled. "Good to see you again."

Shayla was ready for the charade to be over. "What were you doing at the vigil, Jennifer?"

Her eyes grew wide. "Wh-what?"

"The vigil," Tavis supplied. "Two days ago. I saw you there."

"You're mistaken. I wasn't at the vigil. Why would I be at the vigil?"

Tavis took his phone from his pocket and, seconds later, zoomed in on the photo of Jennifer wearing a baseball cap. "That's you in a blond wig. You can't deny it."

"So what were you doing there?" Shayla demanded. "First of all, you lied to me about being sick. Then you're at a vigil for people you don't know?"

"And Shayla and her cousin were run off the road and nearly killed shortly after that vigil." Tavis gave her a stern look. "You'd better start talking."

Jennifer's eyes flitted between them and the front door. She was clearly contemplating a way to escape. She made a little cry.

"You're not going to get far," Tavis told her, "so I suggest you start talking."

"And I'm happy to call the sheriff if you don't want to talk to us," Shayla added. She held up her own phone, making it clear she was ready to punch in the number in a second.

"I'm sorry," Jennifer said.

"Why were you there?" Shayla pressed.

Jennifer looked pained and shifted her weight from one foot to the other. "She's going to kill me."

"Who's going to kill you?"

"I…I just went to…see who was in the crowd."

"I need you to start telling me exactly what you're getting at," Tavis said. "Who's going to kill you?"

"Jenae."

At the mention of her name, both Tavis and Shayla shared a look.

"Jenae?" Shayla asked.

"Yes. Jenae."

Shayla looked toward the back door. She didn't want her mother hearing any of this in case she woke up. "Can we speak outside? I don't want to wake my mother or worry her with anything we're talking about."

Jennifer crossed her arms over her chest and nodded tightly. "Yes."

She sounded pained, terrified. But all three of them went to the back deck. They stood, neither of them taking a seat.

"You're working for Jenae?" Tavis surmised.

"Kind of."

"Where is she?" he asked. "I need to speak with her."

"That's the thing. I haven't heard from her in over a week."

"You just said that you went to the vigil because of her."

"Yes. Because I hadn't heard from her. Because I'm worried about her. When she wouldn't get back to me, I wondered if maybe she would show up at the vigil. I didn't know. So I went, hoping to find her. I've been out of my mind with worry."

Shayla held up a hand. "Whoa, wait a second. You're saying you haven't heard from Jenae?"

"No. Not since last week."

"I'm gonna need you to back up and tell me this story from the beginning," Tavis said. "How did you end up working for Shayla's mother?"

Her shoulders drooped. "I'm a real nurse, if that's what you're wondering. It just so happens that I'm friends with Jenae. In Buffalo. She knew your mother was sick, she'd heard about her cancer. And then when the call came to this agency for a nurse, I pulled a few strings and got this job."

"Why?" Shayla asked. She felt betrayed.

"I want you to know I've been doing nothing but giving your mother the proper care she needs."

"But why did you want to be here? What was so important about working for my mother?"

Jennifer whimpered softly. "Because Jenae said you probably have something here in the house. Something that can help her."

"Me?" Stunned, Shayla stared at Jennifer for a long moment. "Jenae and I weren't even close. How could I have anything that could help her? And help her *what*?"

"It has to do with the murders," Jennifer said. "Obviously," she added when she saw the looks on Shayla's and Tavis's faces. "She was concerned about Lucas."

"Has she heard from Lucas?" Tavis asked.

"She just said that there's some proof somewhere, proof of what Lucas did. And if I could find it, it could help her. So I...I came here. Because she thinks... She feels certain that Lucas gave it to you."

Shayla shook her head. "Lucas gave me nothing," she said. "I don't know why everyone thinks that I was so important to him that he would share any of his criminal plan with me. Why would he?"

"Jenae wasn't certain exactly what I should be looking for. She just said I would know it when I found it."

The nurse's words hit Shayla like a ton of bricks. And she suddenly realized why she'd thought she'd seen things in her room out of place. At first she'd thought she had been imagining things, but now it made sense.

"You were in my room? Going through my things?"

Jennifer started to cry softly. "I was trying to help Jenae. You would do the same to help a friend."

"That's where you're wrong," Shayla said. "I would never lie and sneak around and access someone's private property to help someone else. You could have just come to me and been honest. Instead, you got to my mother as a way to get to me."

"I never hurt your mother. I've given her nothing but amazing care."

"What is it Jenae is looking for?" Tavis asked. "If she asked you to find evidence, you must know."

"She didn't say exactly. Just that I would know it when I saw it. A letter, a gun… I don't know."

"A gun?" Shayla gasped. "You think Lucas gave me a gun?"

"I know it sounds like I'm lying, but I'm not. I think Jenae wasn't sure, just grasping at straws."

"You don't sound like you know much for someone with an agenda who's gained access to private property and private citizens." Tavis's look was unwavering. "You realize we can call the sheriff right now, have you arrested."

"I didn't hurt anybody. I was only trying to help."

"Where were you after the vigil?" Tavis asked. "Because I saw you take off behind the school, as though you didn't want to be seen by anyone. Did you go to a waiting vehicle, one that was stolen? Did you follow Shayla and Deedee and force them off the road? Are you the one who nearly killed them both?"

"No!"

"Then why were you there, and why this whole

subterfuge?" Tavis asked. "Because I don't believe that you were at the vigil looking for Jenae. That doesn't make sense."

"I'm not lying."

"But you did lie to me," Shayla said. "You accessed my house, you went through my things, and did you find anything?"

"No. I didn't find anything useful."

"Does Jenae want Shayla dead?" Tavis asked.

Jennifer's eyes widened. "No. Of course not."

"What do you know about the attack on Shayla in Buffalo?" Tavis pressed on. "Is Jenae working with Lucas?"

"What attack on Shayla?"

Tavis filled her in. "One of the neighbors asked us if we were looking for Jenae. Shayla was lured there, someone tried to kill her—*us*—in a house where Jenae lived. Now we find out you're here working on Jenae's behalf. So tell me, why does Jenae want Shayla dead?"

"She doesn't! She's never said such a thing. She's only said that Shayla probably has some information that can help her."

"Are you denying that Jenae lived at that house in Buffalo?" Tavis asked.

"No," Jennifer said. "But... Maybe her ex found her and that's why she took off. Jenae's relationship with Alex was volatile. She didn't want him knowing where she was. Or...or someone might be setting her up. I'd ask her, but I can't find her."

"That's all you know?" Shayla asked. "Or that's all you're going to tell us?"

"I've told you the truth about everything," Jennifer said. "I swear."

"Good," Shayla said. "Now leave. And never come back."

"Wait," Tavis said. "You mentioned Jenae's ex. I heard that Jenae changed her name so he couldn't find her. What's her new name?"

"She only changed her surname. But I don't think—"

"What is it?" Tavis asked.

"Taylor," Jennifer admitted, her voice barely audible.

"Jenae Taylor," Tavis said. "I'm gonna need her number."

The nurse whimpered. "She won't want me to give you her number."

"Do you want me to call the sheriff?" Tavis countered.

Jennifer angrily brushed a tear away. "Fine. I'll give you her number."

She opened up her phone, found the number and rattled it off.

"Now, what's her connection to Erie, Pennsylvania?" Tavis asked.

"Erie… I think she mentioned having a friend there."

"She never mentioned that she was going there?"

Jennifer shook her head. "No. I don't know anything else." Then she looked at Shayla. "I'm sorry about all of this. I don't expect you to let me stay on."

"How very astute of you," Shayla said.

"I'm sorry," Jennifer repeated. "I really am."

"I'm going to have to call the agency," Shayla said. "You've breached my confidence, and my mother will need another nurse."

Jennifer started for the back door. "Fine. Do what you have to do."

Then she whizzed into the house, grabbed her belongings and was out the front door in a flash. Shayla wanted to follow her, but what would that get her?

Tavis placed a hand on her arm. Shayla looked up at him. "You said you and Jenae were never close. But do you think she hated you because of what happened to Hayley and Jonathan? This nurse was in your house because of her. And she doesn't have answers that make sense to me. And now Jenae is missing. Maybe she went off the deep end, wanted you out of the way for some reason. Maybe she blames you for what happened to Hayley—it could be as simple as that. Or Jonathan. Maybe she's been holding a grudge all this time, saw an opportunity and took it."

Shayla shuddered. "We have to find her. And we have to find her fast."

Chapter Fourteen

Tavis wasn't sure if he should have let the nurse go, but he'd gotten the make and model of her car, plus the license number. He'd have a way to track her down if need be in the future.

He didn't know exactly what was going on here, but something suddenly occurred to him.

"Shayla," he said softly. She was sitting on her sofa, a faraway expression on her face. "Hey, this isn't your fault."

"Isn't it?" Shayla asked, meeting his eyes. "I brought her into my house. I allowed her to be close to my mother."

"But you couldn't have known. How could you have? Their plan was genius. How could you or anyone ever suspect them? Yes, Jennifer got close to your mother, but you can't blame yourself for something that you couldn't have even anticipated."

"But maybe I should have anticipated that coming back here was going to put my mother at risk. My cousin at risk."

Tavis got up from the armchair and joined her on

the sofa. He slipped an arm around her shoulders. "Don't do this."

He stroked her hair softly, and she folded her soft, feminine body against his. And, God help him, he wanted to stay here with her like this, simply holding her and making her feel safe. What had gotten into him?

He cleared his throat, trying to force himself to stop thinking of her as a beautiful and desirable woman. "You said that Lucas asked you about leaving town with him."

"Yes." Shayla angled her face to look up at him. "And Jennifer's comments made me think of something else. I'm pretty sure he mentioned something about having a stash of cash and an insurance policy…? I didn't know what he meant at the time, except that he had money and that we could live off of that when we left. But now I'm wondering if he meant something else."

"There's got to be *something* to be found somewhere. I don't know what it is, but you had more than one person ask you about it, and now Jenae is trying to find something that you allegedly could have? Lucas must have left something somewhere. I don't know what, and I wish I could talk to Jenae to get an answer. But something is somewhere."

"But where?" Shayla asked. "It's not here. Jennifer said she went through my stuff—" She shuddered again, and Tavis knew that she was thinking about the nurse violating her privacy. "So, where?"

"Where he was living. With his aunt and uncle."

"You think so?"

"It's worth a shot, isn't it? All I know is that when Lucas disappeared, his aunt and uncle experienced wrath from the town. I don't know that the sheriff's department interviewed them with any compassion, and the way they've kept to themselves since, I'm thinking not. Maybe it's time I pay them a visit and ask them these very questions. Maybe…" Tavis's voice trailed off. Then his eyes lit up. "Maybe Lucas was afraid of something. You said he seemed on edge. Maybe there's something he knew, something he was worried about…"

"What are you thinking?"

"I don't know," Tavis said, making a face. "All this time we've believed Lucas is the killer. But what if he's a witness?"

TAVIS WAS DETERMINED to get to the bottom of this. If there was any such evidence of an insurance policy anywhere, the best place for it to be would be his aunt and uncle's home. Unless it was stashed somewhere else. But if Shayla didn't have it, he needed to get to Rosita and Andrew's and have a look around.

Was it possible that Lucas had been a witness? He wasn't sure. He wasn't even sure what he was trying to find.

He drove to the Carrs' place, a modest older house in the middle of town, and went to the door. When he knocked, Andrew opened within seconds, as if he'd seen him approaching. The man looked at him with suspicion.

"Hello, again," Tavis said. "I'm wondering if

you would mind if I ask you some questions about Lucas?"

Rosita appeared then, standing beside her husband. "We have nothing else to say about Lucas," she said, her tone defensive. "Everyone crucified him in this town years ago. Aren't you done yet?"

"That's the thing," Tavis said. "I'm wondering... Maybe Lucas wasn't the killer. Maybe he was a witness?"

"What's brought about this change in thinking?" Andrew asked. The edge to his voice said he didn't trust Tavis.

"A few things have happened, and it has me questioning the big picture. Some things just don't make sense."

"Lucas killing anyone doesn't make sense," Andrew said. "We tried to say that in the beginning. That we knew Lucas would never hurt anybody. No one believed us."

"May I come in?" Tavis asked. "I promise I want to hear everything you have to say. If no one ever listened to you before, I'm sorry for that. But I'm prepared to listen to you now."

SHAYLA HAD WANTED to go with Tavis to the Carrs' place, but she'd had to stay behind to wait for the replacement nurse. And it was probably a good thing that she hadn't accompanied him. She was starting to get too used to him being around. Every time she was upset, he was there to turn to. He was like an anchor in a raging sea.

It was clear that she wasn't going to be able to get

through this crisis without him. And what about afterward? That was what she was beginning to fear. How would she go back to her old life now that she'd shared a special moment with him? It may not have meant anything to him, but it meant a lot to her.

The arrival of the new nurse, Kathy, had her putting thoughts of Tavis on the back burner. Kathy was a heavyset woman in her fifties, and she seemed both pleasant and no-nonsense.

Shayla gave her the general rundown of her mother's situation. "Though, of course, you must have all of this information in her file," Shayla added after she'd spoken.

"I'll give your mother the best possible care," Kathy told her. "I'll make sure to get her up and moving. Help her through this."

"Thanks so much."

As Shayla let the new nurse get acquainted with her mother, she called her cousin. "Deedee, how are you?"

"I am doing very well for someone who shouldn't be alive," Deedee said.

"Don't joke about that."

"I'm feeling great. I mean, I've got some pain, but nothing serious, all things considered. And of course my mother is doting on me. I probably gained another five pounds in the past couple of days."

"Good. I'm glad to hear that." She filled her cousin in on what had happened with the nurse, and the fact that Jenae had actually been behind it. "She thinks that Lucas left something for me, some kind of proof. But proof of what, I don't know."

"That's what she said?"

"Yeah. She said that it would be something that could help Jenae. I have no clue what she could be talking about, and there was nothing in my house."

"That is totally creepy."

"Tell me about it. But you know, it got me thinking. Lucas seemed a little bit skittish before the murders. Like he was afraid of something. He didn't tell me what, but he did ask me if I would leave town with him, and he talked about having money and an insurance policy... I didn't know what he'd meant, but Tavis is wondering if it means he *did* leave something here. He's wondering if maybe Lucas wasn't a killer, but may be a witness."

"How does that make sense?" Deedee asked.

"I don't know. We're grasping at straws."

"This whole thing is giving me a headache," Deedee said. "You don't think Lucas is back in town...that he's the one who ran us off the road?"

"If he got away with murder and has been able to avoid the law all these years, why would he risk coming back to town now? Tavis is wondering if maybe Jenae is behind the car accident. Honestly, I don't know. But the crazy thing is, Jennifer said she hasn't heard from Jenae in over a week. Tavis said he got word that she's missing. But you spoke to someone who spoke to her... Right?"

"Yeah," Deedee said. "I relayed the message to you just as it was told to me."

How was it that Deedee had been able to get a message to Jenae when even her parents couldn't reach her? "Who did you contact?" Shayla asked.

"What?"

"You said you got a message to Jenae through a mutual friend. Who is that friend?"

The sound of Deedee's indignant chuckle filled the phone line. "What is this, Shayla?"

"A simple question."

"It sounds to me like you don't trust me."

"There's something else that happened," Shayla said. "I didn't tell you before because Tavis wanted to keep it quiet. But Lucas called me—or someone pretending to be Lucas—and asked me to meet him at a house in Buffalo. I went there thinking I was going to get answers. Instead, Tavis and I were shot at. In a house where Jenae once lived. So if you have a way to reach her via a mutual friend, you can see why I'd like to know."

"Shayla, I'm so sorry. Oh my God. I... Okay, I'm going to tell you this and please don't be mad. I didn't really talk to anyone who talked to Jenae. I...I just wanted you to drop all of this, because I was worried about you."

"So you *lied*?"

"To protect you. Yes."

So Tavis had been right all along. Deedee hadn't been truthful. "Protect me from what?"

"You just told me you were shot at. Maybe if you let all of this go, forget the past, whoever wants to hurt you will move on."

"If only there were a guarantee of that. Anyway, Tavis is at the Carrs' place right now. He's thinking that if there was something that Lucas left behind, it might be there."

"After all these years?" Deedee sounded doubtful.

"It's worth a shot. This whole thing is one giant mystery and, until we solve it, I'm not going to know who's after me. And we need to find that out, because the last thing I want is for you, my mother or anyone else I love to get hurt. And of course I don't want to get hurt either."

"Keep me posted," Deedee said.

"Of course."

"LUCAS CAME TO live with us because he'd been getting into some trouble in Buffalo," Rosita said. "My sister-in-law was at her wit's end and knew that he needed a change."

"So we agreed to let him come live here," Andrew said.

"Lucas might have always found trouble," Rosita began, "but he was always a follower. You know, the type of kid who wanted to look tough. He followed the crowd, did what they were doing, but he was never the instigator. The idea that he would shoot anybody, and especially over some dance competition squabble, was completely ridiculous. I knew it wasn't true."

"He was selling drugs, right?" Tavis asked.

"If he was, it was a small amount," Rosita said. "He wasn't a big-time drug dealer."

Tavis wondered how much Rosita would know. Kids weren't honest about things when they were involved in illegal activities.

"Was he ever in any other trouble?" Tavis asked. "Did he hang out with other kids who were in trouble, or have meetings with people you didn't recognize?"

"Only those guys from school. I never liked them. Especially the Thompson boys. Chase and Alex. He was always with them, out late, drinking. Smoking pot. I always thought they were trouble. Spoiled. Always pulling some kind of prank, from what I heard from Lucas. I told him to limit his time with them, but he was always attracted to the bad ones. And Jonathan too. They always hung out together."

Tavis thought about that for a moment. Did Chase and Alex know more than they had let on? They'd been at the party that night. But based on their accounts, they'd left before any conflict had happened. They'd left, and Hayley and Jonathan had stayed behind, and the next thing they knew Hayley and Jonathan were dead.

At least, that's the story they'd told.

"Did you notice anything different about Lucas in the days before the murder?"

"No," Andrew said. He looked at his wife. "My wife and I had left town. We'd gone on a cruise." He hung his head low for a moment. "Do I ever regret that now. Had we been here, Lucas never could have had that party here. And whatever happened could never have gone down."

Tavis thought about something that he'd discovered when he was working as a cop. "The forensics team was never able to find evidence of the murders in the house, right? No blood, no bullet casings, nothing?"

"No," Andrew said. "Their theory was that Lucas

gave Hayley and Jonathan a ride home. Remember, Shayla had dropped them off and then left. So Lucas was the one to drive them home, but something happened and instead he drove them to the school and shot them. That's what the police believe. And that he took off after that… Disappeared. There was never a car to test for any evidence."

"All we know is that Lucas was gone," Rosita said, "and they pinned the murders on him. But the more I think about it, maybe he could have left because he was afraid."

"Why do you say that?" Tavis asked.

"I don't know. It was just a feeling I had. When we left for the cruise, he was extra loving. He hadn't been quite so loving when he first got here. He didn't like our tough rules. But before we left, he told us how much he appreciated us, hugged us, really just loved on us. I kind of felt… And Andrew thinks the same now… I kinda think that he was saying goodbye."

"Goodbye." Tavis's eyebrows shot up. "Really? So that could mean he was planning to leave?" That aligned with what Shayla had said about him asking her to leave town with him.

"I don't know," Rosita said. "I wish I knew. All I know is that, in my heart, I don't believe he did what they said he did. But did he witness the murders and leave because he was afraid? That, I can believe."

Family members never believed the worst. They could see their loved one pull a gun on someone and they would still find an excuse to justify what happened. You always had to take a loved one's perspective with a grain of salt.

But Tavis was intrigued by the fact that Rosita had the same general sense that Shayla did. That perhaps Lucas was uneasy before the murders and may have been planning to leave town.

"I'm sure the police looked through your place years ago," Tavis began cautiously, "but I'm wondering if there might be something here that can help Lucas. Maybe some sort of evidence? Something he left behind?"

"We searched the room from top to bottom," Andrew said. "We found nothing. And the police didn't find anything either."

"All the same, would you mind if I had a look around?" Tavis asked.

Rosita and Andrew eyed each other. Perhaps because this was the first time anyone had addressed them with any concern for Lucas, their demeanors had changed considerably from when they'd first answered the door. Gone were the tense shoulders and angry expressions, replaced with a more relaxed posture and genuine curiosity.

"That's fine with us," Andrew said.

He led him upstairs to the room that had been Lucas's. It had a bed with a plain white spread on it, and not much else. There was a chest of drawers and a closet. Posters of Kanye West, Jay-Z and Eminem filled the walls.

"We left his stuff as it was in the drawers and the closet, on the off chance he ever came back. But he never did."

Tavis started to look through the drawers. Socks. Briefs. T-shirts. There were some school notebooks, and he flipped through those but didn't see anything of particular interest. He searched every drawer, looking through all that was there to see if there was anything that might be some kind of proof.

But proof of what? He went to the closet and spent time going through folded jeans, checking pockets, hanging clothes, and when he saw the duffel bag on the floor, he thought he'd hit pay dirt. But the bag contained gym clothes, a binder and a few science fiction books. School stuff. Nothing that led Tavis to believe that there was any sort of proof of anything. And certainly not any insurance policy. This was a typical teen's room.

Tavis stood, his gaze downward as he tried to think of something he might be missing. And that's when he saw it. The piece of wood flooring that seemed to be a smidgen higher than the planks around it. It was hardly noticeable. But maybe it was something?

Secret compartment?

He might well be grasping at straws, but he quickly dropped onto his haunches nonetheless. He tried to pull at the edge. It didn't move. He took out his keys and continued fiddling with the plank. And, lo and behold, after several seconds, the wood panel popped up.

"My goodness," Rosita said. "That's a secret hole in the floor?"

Tavis quickly took a picture before he dug farther into the hole. He soon realized that three pieces of the wood paneling came up. Inside the floor was a cardboard shoebox. He pulled it out and opened it. His eyes widened when he saw the gun and a wad of cash.

"That's a gun!" Rosita exclaimed. "That's been here all this time?"

"You've never seen this before?" Tavis asked.

Rosita shook her head. "No. Of course not."

"We never knew that he had a gun," Andrew said.

Rosita curled into her husband's side, placing a hand over her mouth to hide her horror.

Tavis took more pictures. Then he used a T-shirt from the duffel bag to lift the gun. It was a revolver.

"He couldn't have killed those kids," Rosita said, sounding distressed. "He just couldn't have."

"If he did, this wasn't the weapon," Tavis said.

Rosita's eyes grew wide as she looked at him. "How do you know?"

"Because this is a revolver. The gun that killed Hayley and Jonathan was a pistol." He lifted the wad of cash, which was secured with an elastic band. Hundred-dollar bills. "And I'd say this is about five grand."

"You can't tell the sheriff about this," Andrew said. "No matter what you say about the type of weapon, they'll find a way to tie it to the murders."

"That's not how it works," Tavis said. "They have evidence from the shootings. If this gun doesn't match—"

"You think we trust the police?" Rosita asked. "If they know that a gun and thousands of dollars are here, they'll believe everything they assumed about Lucas is true."

"This could clear him of the murders," Tavis said.

"But implicate him of what else?" Andrew countered. "We let you look around to help Lucas, not to hurt him."

Tavis got to his feet. He knew that he should call this in. Was the gun connected to another crime? But the bigger question was why Lucas would leave town without a gun and without all this cash.

"I think you should let the sheriff know about this," Tavis said. "But I'll let you sleep on it and decide later." Was the cash the insurance policy that Lucas had alluded to? "Can I call you tomorrow?"

"You can call us tomorrow," Andrew said, "but I'm pretty sure we won't change our minds. The people in this town have already vilified Lucas. We don't need to give them any more ammunition."

Shayla couldn't believe it when Tavis filled her in. "A gun and a wad of cash?"

"Yes. I know I should call the sheriff, but the Carrs don't want me to. They don't want Lucas's name further dragged through the mud. If I were still a cop, I'd have no choice but to report this. But they let me go through Lucas's room as a favor—hoping I'd find something to exonerate him, not implicate him. I know they've gone through a lot because of the murder case, but I told them they needed to reconsider. What if the gun was used in another crime?"

"There's not a lot of crime in this town," Shayla said.

"Maybe not here, but in Buffalo. Although…" Tavis's voice trailed off.

"What are you thinking?"

"Remember the summer before the murders? There was an old guy who'd been shot downtown. The Elm Street murder."

"That's right," Shayla said. "That case was never solved?"

"No, never. The old guy, Norman Harris, had no known enemies, and certainly no reason to be gunned down. He was in his late seventies, a widower. Took a walk downtown every morning to stay in shape."

"I remember," Shayla said. "His twin granddaughters were high school freshmen."

"All leads went nowhere. In the past, I wondered if possibly the two separate murders could be connected. But Harris's killing seemed entirely random, senseless. Hayley and Jonathan were teenagers who were allegedly killed after an unknown argument— people believed it was about the dance competition, or perhaps something else that went wrong at the party."

"Two entirely different killings," Shayla said.

"I'm going to do some digging, see if I can find out the weapon used to kill Harris. I expect Sheriff Thompson to throw up roadblocks. He wants simple answers to the problems in this town, and if something can't be solved, he's happy to let it go. I'll have to go around him, but if it turns out that Harris was killed with a revolver, maybe Lucas's gun can be checked against that… I'm thinking out loud now, but this is starting to feel right."

"Surely, Sheriff Thompson would want to solve this case," Shayla said.

"You don't know him like I do. And if I'm the one who brings this to him, he most certainly will ignore the issue at hand."

"Why?" Shayla asked.

"This is going to sound crazy, and petty, but it's the truth. It has to do with the sheriff's wife. Ex-wife."

"His wife?"

"She was a 9-1-1 dispatcher, so I knew her. We talked. Were friendly. There was a time that she and the sheriff were having problems. I didn't know that, and she was suddenly hitting on me. She even hired me for protection, allegedly from him, although she didn't specify that at the time. She was quite a bit older than me, but that didn't stop her interest. When I understood what was going on, I let her know that I didn't reciprocate her feelings. But the sheriff saw me as making a play for his wife. Nothing I said to him got through to him. And that's why he hates me. He sees me as being the cause of the end of his marriage."

"That is crazy," Shayla said. "What ended up happening?"

"I passed her off to someone else in my agency, and she wasn't happy. Eventually she canceled the protection contract. She left the sheriff and ultimately remarried. She's still in town. I see her from time to time, and she pretends I don't exist. That's fine by me."

"It seems a bit immature for the sheriff to ignore anything you have to tell him about a case just because of that."

"It is immature. But if I say black, the sheriff says white. Whatever I tell him, I think he deliberately ignores. So I'm going to investigate what I can about the Elm Street murder, see what I can find. Then I'm going to talk to the Carrs and see if I can get them to turn over the evidence. That's the best I can do."

Chapter Fifteen

Shayla called Deedee and filled her in. "I can't believe it, but Tavis found a gun at Rosita and Andrew's place. And get this... It's not the gun that killed Hayley and Jonathan."

"How could he know that?"

"Because it's a revolver. Hayley and Jonathan were shot with a pistol. And get this... He's wondering if maybe this gun was used in another crime. Remember, there was an old guy who was killed the summer before Hayley and Jonathan and no one ever found out who did it? The Elm Street murder."

"Yeah, Mr. Harris. I remember. You think Lucas was the one behind that?"

"I...I would hate to think so. It would mean I knew him even less than I thought I did. It's all premature—maybe the gun isn't related at all. But maybe we're getting closer to figuring this out."

"So what about an insurance policy?" Deedee asked. "Did Tavis find anything like that there?"

"The cash, he's thinking. But Tavis makes a great point. If Lucas left town, why would he leave five grand worth of cash there? And the gun? Nothing about that makes any sense."

"I don't know. But maybe you should just stop all of this. I don't know where this is leading. Lucas left. He never came back, obviously. He's the one who killed Hayley and Jonathan. The fact that there was a gun at his place shows that he was a bigger criminal than we ever thought. Don't you think? Maybe when he killed Hayley and Jonathan he had to take off quickly. That's why he had to leave the money."

That was likely, Shayla couldn't deny it. But still. She didn't know what to make of it all, but the idea that Jenae had been looking for some sort of proof had her feeling like Tavis had just unearthed something important.

"Shayla, I think you need to stop looking into this stuff. Immediately. Someone wants to hurt you. If it's connected to the Elm Street murder, do you really want to be digging into something that could get you killed?"

Shayla made a face. "You say that as if you think that's the scenario. But how could you know that?"

Deedee hesitated a moment. "I'm not saying that I do know that. I'm just… This is a lot. Tavis keeps digging, you keep asking questions and you're going to make someone angry. It's common sense."

"I made someone angry before I even got back here. Someone wanted to hurt me before I started asking any questions."

"Shayla, I love you. But your stubborn streak is too much. You need to stop. Stop asking questions and putting yourself in harm's way."

As Shayla ended the call with her cousin, she couldn't help wondering why Deedee's suggestion seemed more like a warning as opposed to a general concern.

Did her cousin know something that she wasn't telling her?

THE NEXT MORNING, with Griffin outside the house and the nurse tending to her mother, Shayla decided that she should go see Rosita and Andrew. She could share what she had known about Lucas, and get their perspective. She kept coming back to the idea that Jenae was looking for some sort of proof, some sort of insurance policy. Maybe it was somewhere else in the Carrs' house?

But when Shayla drove onto their street, she saw the fire trucks and smoldering smoke in the distance.

Was it...? Her heart leaped to her throat.

And as she got closer, she saw the devastating truth.

The house that had been Rosita and Andrew's no longer existed. It had burned to the ground.

WHEN TAVIS SAW Shayla's name flashing on his phone's screen, he quickly answered the call.

"Tavis!" she cried before he could speak. "They burned down the Carrs' place. They burned it down!"

Tavis shot up in his bed. "The house is burned down?" he asked for clarification, his groggy brain coming to life.

"I just drove by there. I wanted to go see them.

There are fire trucks everywhere. The house is completely gutted. I don't even know if they're okay!"

"Where are you now?" Tavis asked.

"I'm outside the Carrs'."

"Where's Griffin?" Tavis asked.

"He's behind me. He followed me here."

"Go home." He reached for the T-shirt on the chair beside his bed. "Go home and I'll meet you there."

THIS WASN'T A COINCIDENCE. Just yesterday, Tavis had found the secret compartment at the Carrs' place. Now, before he'd even been able to alert the police or turn over the evidence, the house had burned down.

That meant somebody knew something. But who? Shayla was the only one who Tavis had spoken to about what he'd found.

As he drove up to her place, she came out to meet him. He unlocked his vehicle and she hopped into the passenger seat. She looked shaken.

"How did this happen?" she asked. "And why now?"

"That's exactly what I want to know," Tavis said. "This isn't a coincidence." Other things that happened had been possibly coincidental, but this was deliberate. "Who would know that I went to the house?"

Shayla hesitated. Then she said, "I only spoke to Deedee. But Deedee knows the situation."

"Deedee." Tavis said her name through clenched teeth. "You told Deedee?"

"Yes."

"You told her what I found?"

"Yes. But Deedee is my cousin… She was nearly killed in that accident. Why wouldn't I tell her?"

The vein in Tavis's temple began to pound. First, there was the alleged message from Jenae that Deedee had received at a time when no one else had heard from her. Now, Deedee was the only other person who knew what Tavis had found at the Carrs' place—and it had burned to the ground.

"Something's not right here. And unless you went and told somebody else, we have to consider that Deedee was the one who talked to someone."

"No! She wouldn't."

"How do you explain this fire?" Tavis asked. "Just a coincidence the day after I find evidence there? Evidence that I don't even get to turn over to the police? Any connection between that gun and the Elm Street murder or any other unsolved case is now gone."

"Deedee knows what's at stake. Are you trying to tell me you think Deedee's involved in this?"

"Call her. Ask her if she told anyone else."

Shayla looked at Tavis and gasped. "You want me to call my cousin and essentially accuse her of sabotaging this case? You think she also wants to see me hurt, or worse? It doesn't make any sense."

"Call her."

Shayla dialed her cousin. She put the phone on speaker.

"Hey," Deedee said.

"Deedee, I'm here with Tavis. The Carr place burned to the ground last night. You're the only one that I talked to about what was found there. And he's wondering…" Shayla's voice trailed off. She made a face before continuing. "You told me yesterday that I should drop this. Stop looking into this. What did you mean?"

Tavis's eyebrows shot up. So, Deedee *did* know something.

"What are you asking me?" Deedee asked.

"Deedee," Tavis said, "if you know something, this isn't the time to stay quiet. You need to tell me."

"What can I possibly know?" Deedee asked. But there was a higher pitch to her voice, and Tavis didn't believe her.

"Why did you tell me to stop looking into this?" Shayla asked. "If you know something, please tell me."

"It's…common sense," Deedee finally said. "I was nearly killed, remember? The more you ruffle feathers, the more someone's going to be upset. I just… I don't want anything to happen to you."

"Did you talk to anyone about this?" Tavis asked, direct.

Deedee hesitated a beat. "No. Of course not."

She was lying. He couldn't prove it, but he knew it in his gut.

Shayla ended the call and turned to Tavis. "See? My cousin wouldn't do this. She was nearly killed, remember? Now you're acting as though she possibly could be helping whoever wants to hurt me."

"I'm trying to figure this out. Deedee's the one you spoke to about this—unless there's someone else and you're not saying."

A flash of hurt streaked through Shayla's beautiful brown eyes. "Do you really believe that? After all that I've been through, you think I wouldn't tell you the truth now?"

"I have to ask."

She placed her hand on the door handle and pulled. "Of course you do. Because no matter what we've been through, you don't trust me. You never did."

She hopped out of the vehicle and took off toward the house.

No SOONER WAS Shayla in the house, her phone whistled, indicating she'd received a text. It was from Deedee.

Stop looking into this. I can't tell you how I know, but they're angry. You won't be safe if you keep looking.

Shock hit Shayla like a tidal wave. Deedee knew something!

She quickly called her cousin. "Deedee, what are you saying?"

"I don't want to talk about it on the phone. But just know… You're not safe. You gotta let this go. In fact…I think I might go away for a couple of days."

"Deedee, tell me more. You have to."

"If you know what's good for you, you'll stop asking questions. If you stop asking questions, I think they'll let it go. But if you don't…"

"Deedee, I'm your cousin. You can't… You can't leave me hanging like this." Tavis was right. Deedee had been hiding something.

"Okay, I'll tell you this. Lucas…Lucas is dead. He

wasn't the one that called you to the house in Buffalo. He's been dead since the night of the murders. There weren't two casualties that night. There were three. Hayley, Jonathan *and* Lucas."

Shayla was stunned. All these years later and now her cousin was telling her this? How could she ever have kept it from her?

"How come they never found his body?" Shayla asked.

"Because he needed to be the one who took the fall for killing Hayley and Jonathan. You just have to listen to me. I don't want to say any more over the phone."

"Where's his body?" Shayla asked.

Deedee didn't answer right away. "Somewhere it'll be impossible to find."

"Impossible?"

"Not unless someone knows where to look. Probably a hundred kids have been there since and wouldn't know."

"Wait, what are you saying?" Shayla asked.

"I've said enough. Too much. Please, stop this. Stop looking. Let it go."

The line went dead, and Shayla slumped onto the sofa, unable to believe what she'd just heard.

Lucas was dead. He had been since the night of the murders.

He himself had been a victim.

She had to tell Tavis. So she went back out to his truck. When he saw the look on her face, his own face morphed with concern.

She climbed into the vehicle. "What is it?" he asked.

"I think you're right. About Deedee. She…she…" Shayla could barely get the words out, her chest was suddenly feeling tight. It was hard to draw in breath.

"Calm down," he told her. "Breathe in slowly."

She did as he said, calming herself.

"Deedee said…Lucas is dead. He has been since the night of the murders. She said that he was a victim. Just like Hayley and Jonathan."

"Get her on the phone."

Shayla called her cousin. But Deedee didn't answer.

"Of course." Tavis cursed. "This makes total sense. No wonder I couldn't find Lucas anywhere. Not a shred of evidence about the man over the last nine years. Because he wasn't alive."

"I can't believe it," Shayla said.

"If Deedee told you that, she knows who did the killings. Do you think… You think she was involved?"

"Absolutely not. My cousin… She wouldn't…" But what did Shayla truly know? No. She knew her cousin wouldn't be involved in the killing of anyone. Somehow she must have solved the crime on her own, and now was afraid for her life.

Shayla called Deedee again. Again, the phone went to voicemail.

"Now she's ignoring you," Tavis said.

"She begged me to stop looking into this because she said *they* are getting angry. She said if I keep looking into it, my life will truly be in danger."

"Your life is already in danger."

"She's afraid, Tavis. So afraid that she's going to take off for a few days."

Tavis looked at her, and she could see the doubt in his eyes. "I know you can find out where your cousin is. And when you do, you need to tell me."

"That's all she said. I'll try to keep reaching her, but I can't make any promises."

Several hours later, when Shayla still couldn't reach Deedee, she called Tavis and told him exactly that. And she realized then the big mistake she'd made by turning to him for comfort.

"I think you're protecting your cousin," he told her. "She's been lying to me from the beginning. She doesn't want me to know where she is, and you're protecting her."

"After all of this, after everything I've told you, you think I would protect Deedee."

"She's involved in this, Shayla. You know she is. But she's your cousin. Families go to incredible lengths to protect family members even when they're guilty of the most heinous of crimes."

"So you think Deedee is responsible for the murders and that I'm protecting her. That I know where she is and I'm not telling you. You think someone ran me and Deedee off the road and, despite Deedee nearly dying, that was all...what? A well-orchestrated plan?"

"Maybe it was. Maybe it went wrong and Deedee got hurt."

Shayla's mouth fell open. "I can't believe you would say that to me. Deedee wouldn't risk getting herself killed. And she definitely wouldn't try to get me killed."

Ending the call with Tavis, Shayla felt crushed. She thought that she had garnered some trust with Tavis since returning to town. Foolishly, she'd slept with him, thinking that they had reached a new level of understanding.

But the only thing that mattered to him was solving Hayley's murder. She was just a tool to do so.

Shayla needed to finally take matters into her own hands. She'd been trusting Tavis to get to the bottom of this. But her cousin's life was at stake, as was hers. It was time she turned to proper law enforcement.

So the next morning she dug out the card the sheriff had given her. She called him.

"Sheriff Thompson? I have some news for you."

Chapter Sixteen

The next morning, Tavis went to Shayla's door briefly before leaving. He asked her if she'd heard from Deedee, and she told him no. But her voice had been devoid of emotion and her answer so instant that he wasn't sure he believed her.

She was protecting her cousin. She had to be.

Deedee knew more than she was saying, obviously. But she loved Shayla, so why give her half answers? Wouldn't she tell her more details so Shayla could be prepared for whatever danger she was referring to? Why be vague?

Unless Deedee was protecting herself.

And Shayla must have realized that, which is why she wasn't forthcoming about her cousin's whereabouts.

Tavis left Griffin at the house, as he needed to follow up on this lead. He found out that Rosita and Andrew were staying at a hotel, and he went to pay them a visit.

Though he'd already gotten word of the initial finding of arson at the scene, the Carrs shared the details of their harrowing experience. They'd been asleep when they'd heard the fire crackling, and had barely made it out of the house without being overcome by smoke. Someone had doused the entire outside of the house with gasoline, and also had broken some windows and thrown gasoline inside to ensure the fire quickly engulfed the house. The fact that they'd made it out with their lives and no injuries had been a miracle. Andrew's quick thinking to wear their winter coats had saved them from being burned.

"And the evidence?" Tavis asked. "Was it still in Lucas's room?"

"We left it where we found it. Everything's gone."

Tavis left the Carrs and called Deputy Jenkins. "Where are you?" he asked the man without preamble.

"At Molly's Café, getting a muffin and a coffee. Why?"

"Can I see you? This is urgent."

"I'll wait here. How long will you be?"

"Give me five minutes."

When Tavis arrived at Molly's, he saw Deputy Jenkins standing outside his vehicle. He was speaking with a middle-aged couple, and Tavis approached slowly. Jenkins saw him, nodded, and then Tavis joined the man at his cruiser as the couple walked away.

"Maybe we should sit inside your car for this," Tavis told the deputy.

Moments later, they were both seated in the deputy's vehicle. "Obviously, you heard about the fire at the Carr place," Tavis said.

"Yes. Such a shame. It was arson."

"It wasn't a coincidence," Tavis said. "This has to do with Lucas and the murders nine years ago."

"Come on, Tavis. How could it?"

"Because I went to see them the day before yesterday. And I found something in Lucas's room. I found a box with a gun and a wad of cash. There was a secret compartment in the closet floor. Nobody knew about it. Obviously, it was missed by investigators in the past. Someone must've gotten word as to what I'd found. And they torched the place."

The deputy looked doubtful.

"Come on, you're a cop. You know there's no such thing as coincidence."

The deputy sighed. "Tavis, why is it anything you get yourself involved in ends up getting worse?"

"Spare me Sheriff Thompson's analysis. This situation is getting out of hand because somebody knows I'm getting close." He paused, glancing out at the street as a mother with two young children walked by. Sheridan Falls was an idyllic little town. But there was a dark secret here, one that was finally coming to light.

He turned back to the deputy. "All I have are pictures of the revolver and the cash that I found in the secret compartment. But I was thinking about the Elm Street murder, how that was never solved. I'm wondering what type of gun was used to kill Norman Harris. Because if it was a revolver…"

"If it was a revolver, we'll never know if it was the one at the Carrs' residence."

"Listen to me. There are three murders in this town that need to be solved, and I know you're not like the sheriff. I always thought it was probably some kids who'd killed the old guy, some dumb drunken activity. Or maybe an initiation. Rosita and Andrew said that Lucas hung out with Alex and Chase and Jonathan. They said they always thought Alex and Chase were no-good influences on their nephew. I'm thinking now that maybe Alex and Chase know more than they ever told me."

Deputy Jenkins glanced around, as though making sure no one was within earshot even though they were behind the closed doors of his cruiser. "You didn't hear this from me. But years ago, there was some speculation that Alex and Chase were involved in that shooting. The Elm Street murder."

"You're kidding."

"But the idea was quickly dismissed. They're the sheriff's boys. They wouldn't do anything so heinous. Anyway, it was just a rumor, and the sheriff figured people were just being bad-minded, going after his kids. The whole concept was quickly squashed."

Tavis's gut began to tighten. The gun and the cash at the Carrs' place—the insurance policy? It made sense. "So this isn't the first time that someone considered this?"

The deputy shook his head. "No. But just because the idea was thrown out there doesn't mean that they did it. And by your own admission, you found a revolver in Lucas's closet. When he came to this town, he was always known for being a troubled teen. So maybe he killed Hayley and Jonathan and he also killed Mr. Harris."

"There's something else," Tavis said. "And for now, I'd like to keep this between us. But I got word from someone that Lucas is dead. That he was killed the night that Jonathan and Hayley were killed. And if that's true, then he didn't kill them. Someone else did."

Alex and Chase? Tavis wondered.

Deputy Jenkins looked at him with a disbelieving expression. "Who told you that?"

"I can't say right now. But if you can find out and let me know the weapon that was used to kill Mr. Harris, maybe I can finally start putting these pieces together in a real way."

"I don't need to look into the file because I worked the case. The weapon that killed Norman Harris was a revolver."

"Thanks," Tavis said. "I know I'm close, and I'm going to solve this case."

SHAYLA KNEW THAT leaving the house with Griffin watching was going to pose a bit of a problem. So before she got into her car to leave the driveway, she approached his vehicle.

"Hey," she said, forcing a smile onto her face. "I'm just running to the store for a few minutes. Maybe ten, fifteen. I'd really appreciate it if you'd stay here and guard the house, because I'm worried about my mother. Tavis might have told you that we had an issue with the previous nurse and, while I trust this one, I just prefer that someone be here to watch over her. In fact, I'd prefer that you stay in the house."

When Griffin looked slightly concerned at her request, Shayla summoned a tear and forced emotion into her voice. "I'd never forgive myself if anything happened to my mother because of me. Please, stay in the house until I get back. Make sure my mother's safe. I won't be more than ten, fifteen minutes."

"All right," Griffin agreed. "As long as you agree to call me if you need me."

"Yes. I'll absolutely call you if I need you." She dabbed at her eyes and flashed him a soft smile. "Thank you."

She led Griffin into her house, introduced him to the nurse, then got into her car and headed for town.

SHERIFF THOMPSON WAS waiting outside the building when Shayla pulled into the department parking lot. He waved a hand and smiled as she got out of her vehicle.

"Hello, Sheriff Thompson," she said. "I'm glad you could meet with me."

"No problem," he told her. "It sounds like you have something serious to discuss with me."

"I do." She blew out a frazzled breath. "I got word from someone, and I think this makes sense. Lucas Carr is allegedly dead."

The sheriff's eyes grew as wide as saucers. "Dead?"

Shayla nodded. "Apparently murdered. The same night as Hayley and Jonathan. And if that's the case, then that means he didn't kill them. Someone else killed all three of them."

"My God," the sheriff said. "Do you know where the body is?"

"Um, not really." Shayla hesitated. "But, I was thinking about that all night. There's this barn on the outskirts of town. We used to hang out there. Kids would drink, or smoke pot, party. It was a great location because the property was abandoned. If anyone wanted to get rid of a body so that it wouldn't be found, my guess is they'd bury it there."

"Can you show me?" Sheriff Thompson asked.

"I...I guess. Though I'm not sure if his body is there."

"But let's go check it out," the sheriff said. "You could be on to something."

Shayla's phone began to ring. She saw Tavis's name and number flashing on her screen. She rejected the call.

"Ready to go?" Sheriff Thompson asked. "I'll drive, and you can lead me to this barn."

Shayla nodded. She wanted answers as much as the sheriff. "Sure."

TAVIS FROWNED WHEN his call to Shayla bounced to her voicemail almost instantly. He called again, and again the same thing happened.

Was she rejecting his calls?

He understood that she was upset with him, but he needed to talk to her.

Everything made sense now. Alex and Chase were the ones behind the killings of Hayley and Jonathan. Of the guys who used to hang out and cause trouble, only Alex and Chase were still alive. They'd killed Old Man Harris on Elm Street. Maybe Lucas had been involved. Jonathan too. Though they'd all been close, something had happened and they'd ended up killing Jonathan and Lucas. Maybe to silence them as witnesses?

He tried calling Shayla again, and when again the

call went to voicemail after the second ring, he sent her a text instead.

Call me. It's important.

SHAYLA SWIPED TO reject Tavis's call.

"That's Tavis?" the sheriff asked, glancing at her.

"Yes."

"That man acts like he has a thorn in his backside. Always on edge, never letting a situation go."

"Tell me about it," Shayla said softly.

"You did the right thing by coming to me. I'm the sheriff in this town. If what you say about Lucas is true, we'll find his body, and I promise you I will investigate this to the fullest extent and find out what happened to him."

"Thank you. If we can find out who's trying to hurt me, I can finally be free of this."

She scrawled out a text to Tavis.

I'm with Sheriff Thompson. We're going to look for Lucas's body. I'll be in touch later.

Then she turned off her phone.

WHEN SHAYLA'S TEXT came in, Tavis's heart sank. He quickly called, but the phone didn't ring at all. Just went to voicemail. He tried to text her, tell her to not go with the sheriff anywhere, but she didn't respond. He called again, then again. Each time, he was told to leave a message.

He needed to find Shayla. If she was with the sheriff, she was in danger. Because for Alex and Chase to have gotten away with murder all those years ago, they'd had to have help. And who better to help them than the town's top law man, their own father?

Tavis had seen it a million times. Family members going to all sorts of lengths to protect their loved ones from facing justice. Even if that person wore a badge.

How far would the sheriff go to make sure his boys avoided the law?

Tavis didn't want to find out.

He called Deedee's number, and it rang and rang. At least her phone was on. He drove to her house, found her parents there. They confirmed what Shayla had already told him. That Deedee was gone. Said she'd needed to get away for a couple of days; her parents didn't know why.

"If you know where she is, I need you to tell me."

Deedee's parents looked at each other with concern. "What's this about?"

"This is a matter of life and death. I'm worried about Shayla, and I think Deedee's the only one who can help me."

"She told us not to tell anyone where she went."

"Then do me a favor. If you have a way to reach her, call her. Tell her to call me immediately. Let her know that I think that Shayla is right now in mortal danger, and I need her help."

It DIDN'T TAKE more than ten minutes for Tavis's phone to ring. He answered right away. "Tavis Saunders."

"It's Deedee."

"Thank God. Deedee, I don't care what you knew

and when, but I care about finding Shayla. I think she's in danger. She's with the sheriff right now."

Deedee gasped, confirming his suspicion. "So, I'm right. She's not safe with the sheriff."

"Where are they?"

"Shayla said something about going to see if she could find Lucas's body." Tavis paused for a beat. "Tell me everything. Because I know that you know. And you're the only chance I have of finding Shayla."

"If she's with the sheriff, she's in danger. They've been warning me since she got back. Afraid that she was going to get close to the truth."

"Alex and Chase?" Tavis asserted.

"Yes. They killed Jonathan and Lucas because they were in the car when Alex and Chase killed that man on Elm Street. They were getting paranoid, thought that one of them was going to talk. Hayley just happened to be there that night, and they couldn't let her live."

"Where would the sheriff be taking her?"

"All I can think is that Shayla figured out possibly where the body could be buried. I kind of hinted at it, but I wasn't specific. We used to hang out there. You remember the old abandoned barn on the edge of town? Kids would hang out there, party, drink."

"Yes."

"Either she guessed that's where I was talking about when I said Lucas was buried where he'd never be found, or the sheriff suggested taking her there."

"Thank you, Deedee," Tavis said.

"Find her," Deedee said. "Find her before it's too late."

TAVIS QUICKLY CALLED Deputy Jenkins. "Jenkins," he hurriedly said when the man answered the phone. "Shayla's with the sheriff. And I think she's in danger."

"Tavis, come on."

"Hear me out," Tavis said. And then he filled him in. "This is a credible witness, someone I know personally. What she says makes sense. Think about it. You said yourself that Alex and Chase were suspected in the Elm Street murder. But nothing ever came of that. Don't you think it makes sense that Sheriff Thompson covered up their crime? These are his boys. He wasn't going to let them go down for murder."

"I hope you're wrong," Jenkins said.

"Listen, I'm calling you because I need to find Shayla. She and the sheriff are apparently going to the old abandoned barn at the edge of town. I'm heading there now. And I need to know that you have my back. I think he's going to hurt her."

"Damn, this is a mess," Jenkins said.

"Yeah, it is. Can I count on you?"

The deputy exhaled sharply then said, "You can count on me."

THE SHERIFF PULLED his car into the long driveway that led to the abandoned barn. When he stopped and cut the engine, he and Shayla exited the vehicle.

"Show me exactly where you guys used to hang out," he said.

Shayla looked around. This place was still exactly as she remembered it. The peeling red paint. The broken windows, the missing wood panels.

"We used to hang out either in the barn, or sometimes outside of it. It's crazy when I think about it. The stairs leading to the second level in the barn were so unstable, but that didn't stop us from climbing them anyway. Some teens would seek privacy in the old horse stalls and make out." Shayla looked around. "But Lucas wouldn't be in the barn. There's a firepit at the back." Shayla led the way there. "Right there," she said, pointing. "We liked to hang out there too, sometimes roasting marshmallows and making s'mores. This was the perfect place to hang when we were in school. Somewhere we knew we wouldn't get caught."

"And where's Lucas's body?"

Shayla whirled around to look at the sheriff. "I don't know. I just assume it's probably out here somewhere." She looked toward the field behind the barn. The area was vast. "I couldn't begin to tell you. But maybe if you guys get cadaver dogs—" Her voice stopped abruptly when she turned again to look at the sheriff. For a moment, she couldn't register what she was seeing.

And then she did. He had a gun. And he was pointing it at her.

"What are you doing?"

Gone was the smile on his face, replaced with a dark, evil look. "You should've let this go," he said.

Shayla's mouth fell open, her brain scrambling to make sense of the situation. How was this possible? The sheriff wanted to kill her?

"You…you want to kill me?"

"It's not that I want to. But I have to. You were getting too close. Asking too many questions. Putting it all together. Eventually this was going to be a problem."

"I...I don't know what's going on here."

"Oh, I think you do."

Keeping his gun trained on her, the sheriff went to the back of his cruiser, popped it open and removed a shovel. Walking back to Shayla, he tossed it at her. It landed on the ground in front of her feet.

"Pick it up!" he bellowed.

Shayla quickly lowered herself and picked up the shovel.

"Very good," he told her. "Now walk."

When she didn't immediately move, he shoved the gun in her back, and she started to walk. "Where?"

"Toward the well."

Shayla moved one foot in front of the other, heading toward the well that was on the property. Once they had passed the well by about twenty feet, the sheriff said, "That's enough. Stop right there."

She stopped, and looked over her shoulder at him. Her chest was rising and falling with rapid breaths.

"Start digging."

"Is this where Lucas is?" Her voice was a croak.

The sheriff chuckled, a hollow, evil sound. "Oh, you're cute. But since you seem to be continuing to play the innocent act, let me be clear. You're digging a grave. *Your* grave."

Chapter Seventeen

Tavis raced toward the edge of town, his heart in his throat every step of the way. This was his fault. He'd come down hard on Shayla once again, and she had done the one thing that made sense. She'd turned to the sheriff for help. Instead of him.

Because she couldn't trust him.

Couldn't trust him to have faith in her. Couldn't trust him to be there for her.

He mentally chastised himself and promised that if he ever got the chance, he would never fail her again. Deedee had kept her in the dark as well. He would find out later the extent of what had gone on that horrible night nine years ago, but he had painted Shayla with a tarnished brush. The same brush he'd painted her with all those years ago when he'd suspected that she hadn't been honest about Lucas.

He hadn't meant to offend her. He'd just been so desperate to get to the truth.

Too desperate. Desperate to solve the murder of someone who was already dead and gone, as opposed to cherishing a person who was alive and well.

Alive and needed protecting.

And if she died at the hands of the sheriff, this would be on his watch. His responsibility.

Griffin couldn't stop apologizing, but Tavis didn't blame him. This was his fault. He'd sent her running to the sheriff because she couldn't trust him to be there for her.

There was nothing Tavis could have done to protect Hayley, but he could have protected Shayla.

And he'd failed.

"Hold on, Shayla. I'm coming."

He hit the accelerator.

SHAYLA'S BROW DRIPPED with sweat from digging. She didn't understand why the sheriff was doing this. And if she was going to die here, she deserved to know why.

"Why are you doing this?"

"You were going to find out sooner or later, because that cousin of yours couldn't keep her mouth shut. But I couldn't let my boys go to prison. Do you understand? No one meant to kill Hayley. She was just in the way. But Lucas and Jonathan? They were gonna try to take my boys down."

"For what?" Shayla asked.

"You know I'm talking about the Elm Street killing. Now, I never condoned them killing Old Man Harris, but his life had already been lived. My boys were young. Made a stupid mistake. They didn't deserve to lose their lives over something like that."

Alex and Chase… They were behind the Elm Street murder!

How did Jenae fit into this? Had she known? She

must have, just like Deedee. Is that why she'd taken off? Was Jenae even alive?

And then it hit her. Jenae and Deedee had been dating Chase and Alex at the time of the murders.

"Did you kill Jenae too?" Shayla asked.

"If she knows what's good for her, she will never come back to this town. And she'll keep her mouth shut. You are going to be the example to anyone else who thinks that opening their mouth will get them anywhere. It won't. I'm the law in this town. I run things here."

"You don't have to do this," Shayla said. "I won't say anything, I promise."

"You won't, because you'll be dead."

"So if Lucas is dead, who tried to kill me in Buffalo?"

Sheriff Thompson snorted. "Alex messed that up. It would have been the perfect setup. Jenae tried to hide, but he found out where she was living. You were supposed to die there, then everyone would think she'd killed you. With her own murder charge, she wasn't going to be a problem anymore— Who told you to stop? Keep digging!"

Shayla pushed the shovel into the dirt, her chest heaving. What if she swung the shovel backward and whacked the sheriff in the head? Could she hurt him enough to disarm him? Or would he just get angry and then shoot her?

"I can see what you're thinking. But don't. Because if you make me kill you, I won't make your death quick. I'll make you suffer. But if you dig your grave, I'll give you one bullet that will take you out and you won't feel a thing."

"And my mother? You would take me away from her when she needs me?"

The sheriff hesitated, as though for a moment considering his conscience. "This isn't what I wanted. But this is your fault, Shayla. At least now Lucas's insurance policy has been destroyed in the fire and there's nothing tying my boys to the Elm Street murder."

"I promise you, I'll say nothing."

Gone was the sheriff's momentary glimpse of conscience. His expression darkened. "Dig, or I'll make you suffer."

Shayla whimpered and continued to dig.

TAVIS SLOWED DOWN on the road in front of the barn. The last thing he needed was to approach the property with tires squealing and alert the sheriff that he was there. The property was large, but he was hoping that he would be able to find the sheriff and Shayla fairly quickly. He would need stealth and quiet as he advanced.

He parked his Sierra on the road. The sheriff's cruiser was down the length of the driveway. At least the barn was close enough to the road. The field behind it was vast. From memory, he knew there was at least another building back there as well, but they could be anywhere.

He exited his vehicle, got his gun, and cut across the gravel and weeds that led toward the barn. As he made his way around the side of the building, he strained to listen for sound. He heard nothing.

As he got to the back of the barn, he peered out carefully. And in the distance, he saw them. Shayla with a shovel. She was digging. And the sheriff had a gun trained on her.

His back was to Tavis, and so was Shayla's. But damn it, they were a distance off.

There was a thicket of trees to the right. He could go that way and try to get closer.

He took out his phone and opened the camera app. These new phones had amazing capabilities, and his was no exception. He was able to zoom in close enough to capture the sheriff with his gun on Shayla. He took the picture and texted Deputy Jenkins.

I'm at the property right now. The sheriff looks like he's ready to kill Shayla! Here's the proof.

Then he sent the picture.

Now, Tavis needed to get close. At least close enough to take a shot if need be. He went around the other side of the barn toward the thicket of trees at the side. And then, hoping the trees would cover him, he began to advance.

"CAN YOU HURRY it up?" the sheriff said. "I ain't got all day."

Shayla really wished she could take the shovel and pummel this man. How dare he expect her to dig her own grave so that he could kill her, and do it without any complaint? But what could she do? Maybe the best thing to do was to make her move, and then try to run for it. It was her only way…

She felt so stupid now, not trusting Tavis. He had been the one person in this town determined to make sure she was okay. Even her cousin had betrayed her. Whatever Deedee had known, she should have told her a long time ago. It could have spared her this right now.

She couldn't even turn her phone on at the moment without attracting the sheriff's attention. She had stupidly turned it off. There was no way for anyone to find her.

"You don't have to do this. Whatever you think I'm going to say, I won't. Hayley's death was a long time ago. All of this is ancient history. No one needs to worry about it anymore."

"Yeah, but there's something to be said about loose ends. Loose ends and loose lips. I know that your friend Tavis is never gonna let this go. I'm sorry, I genuinely like you. But there's no other way."

"Sheriff Thompson!"

A sense of shock hit Shayla like a sledgehammer to the chest. When she realized the voice wasn't a figment of her imagination, euphoria quickly took hold. She threw her gaze to the right, toward the trees. And then she saw him. Tavis. His gun drawn.

"Tavis Saunders." The sheriff laughed without mirth. "I should've known you'd end up here. But you know what? This is good. Even better than I'd imagined."

Shayla wanted to throw the shovel and run to

Tavis, but the sheriff would shoot her dead in a second.

"Put the gun down," Tavis demanded.

"Really?" Thompson asked. "You're going to tell the sheriff to put the gun down? Not gonna happen. But it's a good thing you came here in time to join your girlfriend. Because now, when she dies, I'll have been here to save the day. You blamed her for Hayley's death, and that's why you killed her. Unfortunately, I'll have no choice but to shoot you dead."

"This is over, sheriff." Tavis spoke firmly.

Shayla didn't know what to do. She only knew that, finally, she felt a sense of hope.

"Drop the gun, Tavis. Kick it over here. Or I'll make your girlfriend suffer."

Tavis held up his phone and, for a moment, Shayla was confused. And then he explained.

"I've already taken a picture of you with your gun trained on Shayla. I sent it to Deputy Jenkins. By the end of this day, everyone in town will know that you're a fraud. We know what happened. We know you covered for Alex and Chase. We know you covered for them killing Lucas. I don't have all the other details, but that's enough. You gotta love technology," Tavis added, chuckling. "There's nothing you can do now to escape this. Everybody in this town is going to know you're a corrupt sheriff who let murders go unsolved and even committed murder to save your boys."

The sheriff's face fell. Shayla gazed at him, wondering if he was going to shoot her. His gun was still on her, but he quickly threw it in Tavis's direction. "You sent a picture?" he asked through clenched teeth.

"The killing stops," Tavis said. "You're not going to kill another person to save your two spoiled sons who you couldn't control."

In the distance, sirens sounded. Shayla's knees buckled and she almost dropped to the ground. These few seconds would be precarious, but she felt a surge of hope. Tavis had come to save the day.

Sheriff Thompson's eyes widened at the sound of the sirens. And as Shayla watched, he did something she didn't expect. He turned the gun from Tavis and put the muzzle in his mouth. Then he fired.

SHAYLA SCREAMED. Tavis ran toward her and scooped her in his arms. She cried, clinging to him, and he clung to her. She was alive. He'd gotten to her in time. Waves of relief washed over him.

"Oh my God, Tavis!"

"Sweetheart," he said, breathing into her hair, inhaling the scent of her just to make sure this moment was real.

"He was going to kill me. I thought I was going to die."

"I told you I would take care of you. I failed for a moment, and I'm sorry for that. But I'm here now."

As he pulled back and looked at her, and brushed away her tears, he brought his mouth down on hers and kissed her fiercely. He wasn't thinking, but feeling. Feeling this incredible sense of relief and something else. Shayla was safe in his arms. And he didn't ever want to let her go.

Two days later, after the dust had settled and the town learned the truth of the horrifying acts that had happened nine years ago and what had almost happened to her, Shayla was finally getting to breathe.

Hayley, completely in the wrong place. Lucas and Jonathan, caught up with the wrong crowd. Alex and Chase—monsters.

At least they'd been arrested, and with their father dead and gone, they were certain to pay for their crimes this time.

Deedee couldn't stop apologizing. She'd come to see Shayla and explain everything. "I was afraid. What more can I say? I thought that being silent was going to protect you, protect me. But they were scared. Totally scared of you being back and finding the proof that Lucas left."

"Why didn't you just tell me? You didn't trust me to keep a secret?"

"They told me that if I ever told anyone, they would kill me and kill my parents. I saw what they'd already done. How could I doubt them?"

"But I never would have betrayed your confidence. You know that."

"But what if just knowing the truth caused you to react somehow differently? Like when you brought your car to Chase? If you'd known he was responsible for Lucas's murder, you might have looked at him differently. Instead, at least when you went to his shop, you were pleasant with him, and he was none the wiser."

"And yet, they still tried to kill me."

"I know. I thought I was doing the right thing."

"You got into the jail to talk to Chase?" Shayla asked. Her cousin had promised she would before she came to see her. To get answers about the recent attacks on her life.

"Alex was the one who stole the SUV and ran us off the road. He was at the vigil and left right when it was over so that he could follow us. Heading to the cemetery gave him the perfect opportunity to try and kill us. I guess he figured if he killed me too, it would make their lives easier. I certainly couldn't tell you anything if I were dead."

"I can't believe them. All these years, they got away with what they did and hung around this town and acted as though I was the evil one."

"But they're going to pay for their crimes now. That's what matters. And you're safe."

Shayla looked at her cousin. So much had happened, so much that was hard to believe.

"I'm sorry," Deedee said, and her voice broke.

Shayla put her arms around her cousin and hugged her. "I know you are. Deedee, I love you. I don't blame you."

Deedee wept, and Shayla held her, the two of them finally able to feel the relief that came from knowing there was no longer a threat to their lives.

TWO DAYS LATER, Tavis approached Shayla's house. He hadn't heard from her, and it was gnawing at him. He knew that a lot had happened and she was dealing with so much. Her cousin, the aftermath of this absolutely crazy ordeal, the emotional distress of everything. Not to mention her mother's illness. But still, he wanted to see her.

She answered the door and looked up at him with those bright brown eyes, her mouth forming an O. How lovely she was.

"Hey, Shayla."

"Hi."

"I know I haven't heard from you, and I understand you might be upset with me. I just wanted you to know that I'm sorry."

"It's okay."

Was it? "I judged you harshly and I shouldn't have."

"But you do that, don't you?" she asked, a tinge of sadness in her voice. "With Hayley, you judged me. And with Deedee, you judged me."

"I was wrong, and I'm sorry. But…what about us?"

"I'll always be grateful that you saved me, but I know that everything that happened between us… We were caught up in the moment. I understand, and I'm at peace with everything."

"What if I don't agree that we were simply caught up in the moment?"

There was sadness in her eyes. "I don't know what I'm going to be doing," she went on. "Probably heading back to Florida. And you'll be staying here. We don't have to have an awkward conversation about what happened. It is what it is, and I'm okay with that. I'm just glad this whole thing has been solved and we can both move forward."

Her words were like a punch to the gut. Had their

one night meant nothing to her? Heck, he didn't know fully what it meant to him. He only knew that he didn't want their relationship to be over.

"I'd like for us to have a conversation at some point," Tavis said. "When things have calmed down."

"Is there any point in prolonging the inevitable?" she asked.

When he said nothing, she continued. "I'm going to see my mother now. Unfortunately..." Her eyes began to well with tears. "Unfortunately, she's taken a turn for the worse."

"Shayla, I'm so sorry."

"Thank you."

She closed the door, and as Tavis walked away from the house, he felt a very odd and distressing sensation deep in his heart.

Epilogue

Two weeks later, the sun was shining bright in the sky and a flock of geese flew overhead just as the crowd finished singing the last verse of "Amazing Grace." Shayla looked at the coffin that had just been lowered into the ground, and dropped her yellow rose onto it. Her mother's favorite.

"Goodbye, Mom."

Deedee hugged her, and Shayla turned into her cousin's arms, holding back her tears. Her mother wouldn't want her to cry anymore. There'd been enough tears already.

This wasn't what she'd wanted for her mother, but the truth was, her mother had been gravely ill, something Shayla hadn't been able to accept until the final days of her life. Shayla would have to cherish the memories and the time she'd shared with her mother these last weeks. She could never regain the time they'd lost, but she knew that her mother was at peace now, in a better place. And she would always be with her.

Her aunt and uncle hugged her, as did others in the crowd. Many of the townsfolk had come out to see Michelle Phillips laid to rest. It was a wonderful send-off.

As Shayla looked up at the cloudless sky, she felt a sense of renewed hope. The mystery was solved. Her name was cleared. Her mother was at rest. And the future ahead of her would no longer be tainted with fear.

With Deedee's arm around her waist, Shayla began to walk away from the grave. She saw someone in the distance in a skirt and sandals walking toward her. A familiar face. Jenae!

Shayla stopped walking, and Jenae came right to her.

"Hello, Deedee, Shayla."

Shayla swallowed. She didn't know if she was happy to see Jenae or not. The fear had been that she'd been killed. "Jenae."

"I'm sorry for your loss," she said, and her face filled with sorrow.

"Thank you," Shayla said.

"I just want you to know, I'm sorry about how everything played out. But I was afraid. You know the story now, I'm sure," she said, throwing a glance at Deedee. "I was married to Alex and I knew exactly how dangerous he was. When I got away from him, I changed my name so that I could be safe. But this murder that happened years ago always hung over my head. I was always afraid that he would kill me because I knew the truth.

"The night of the murders, Lucas mentioned something about an insurance policy. Before they killed him, he said they'd never get away with it because of this insurance policy. We searched high and low, but couldn't find anything, and I finally started to think he may have left it with you. That's why I sent the nurse to your house. What I wanted was proof that I could take Alex down with, so that I could be safe. I never wanted to hurt you."

"I understand now," Shayla said.

"I thought changing my last name would keep me safe from Alex, but he still found me. That's when I went into hiding. I got involved with another guy and he promised he'd protect me, but you can never be sure. I was convinced Alex was going to kill me."

"Shaker?" Shayla asked, remembering the name the guy on the street in Buffalo had mentioned.

"Yes, his real name is Henry. He prefers his street name, though."

"Thank God you got away from Alex," Shayla said. Jenae's story tied up the last loose end. "I can't believe his father..." Shayla's voice trailed off.

"Sheriff Thompson didn't get to hurt you," Jenae said. "That's what matters."

"I know."

Jenae opened her arms, and Shayla accepted the hug she offered. "I can now get back to my life," Jenae said. "And I hope you can too."

Shayla nodded. "That's the plan."

Jenae turned and walked away, and Shayla hugged her cousin a little tighter.

"Have you heard from Tavis?" Deedee asked.

"No," Shayla said. "Look, I know he was being nice to me because he felt a sense of obligation. And he didn't want anything to happen to me, and I'm glad he was there to save my life. But that's all there is to it."

"Are you sure about that?" Deedee asked.

"Of course I am. He never liked me. We just had... a moment."

Deedee's eyes wandered off, and Shayla followed her line of sight. She sucked in a breath when she saw Tavis standing near a tree, dressed in a suit and sunglasses. Looking every bit as incredible as he ever had.

"I think you might be wrong," Deedee said, a smile on her face. And in her voice. Then she stepped away.

Shayla's heart was beating fast as Tavis approached.

As he neared her, his lips pulled into a grin. "It's good to see you, Shayla."

"Likewise," she told him. Why did she feel so flushed suddenly?

His face grew serious. "I was sorry to hear about your mother."

"Thank you."

"I stayed away, because I know you were going through a tough time. And because you were mad at me."

"Tavis, none of that matters now."

"It does matter. Because...I don't know what your plans are, but there's no threat to you here in Sheridan Falls anymore. And this was always your home. You mentioned you have an e-store, so your business is operated online. I'm hoping... Maybe you'll consider staying here?"

"The thought has crossed my mind," she said honestly. With her business online, Lyndsay could still work for her. There were logistics she would need to work out, but it was doable. She'd spent so much time running, and Florida was nice, but it had never felt like home. Here, she could be in the place where she had loved growing up and had spent so many wonderful years with her mother.

"Or maybe you would consider coaching young dancers here. You mentioned once that you'd wanted to coach."

"You seem to have it all figured out," Shayla said.

"I want you here," Tavis said bluntly.

Her breath caught in her throat. He was holding nothing back.

"Shayla, what happened between us wasn't just some isolated moment. There's something special between us, don't you feel it?"

"Yes," she admitted breathlessly. But she'd spent the last couple of weeks telling herself that this couldn't be possible. That Tavis didn't feel anything for her. It was easier than getting her hopes up.

He slipped an arm around her waist and pulled her close. "Stay in Sheridan Falls. Stay with me."

The deep timbre of his voice rumbled through her body, followed by a wave of happiness. She'd always had a crush on him. And now the crush had blossomed into something more…

"Do you really mean it?" she asked.

"Absolutely. I want you here. I want you in my life."

And to prove the point, he lowered his head and kissed her. Softly. Sweetly. A kiss that proved without doubt that there was something special between them.

Something worth staying here and fighting for.

* * * * *

WE HOPE YOU ENJOYED
THIS BOOK FROM

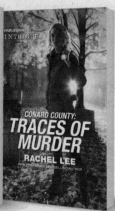

Seek thrills. Solve crimes. Justice served.

Dive into action-packed stories that will keep you
on the edge of your seat. Solve the crime
and deliver justice at all costs.

6 NEW BOOKS AVAILABLE EVERY MONTH!

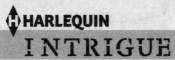
#2097 COWBOY JUSTICE AT WHISKEY GULCH
The Outriders Series • by Elle James

Outrider security agent Parker Shaw and his trusted equine and canine sidekicks are dedicated to safeguarding those in need. Having escaped abduction and imprisonment, Abby Gibson is hell-bent on rescuing the other captives. Trusting Parker is her only option. As danger nears, their choice may come down to saving themselves...or risking everything to save the hostages.

#2098 THE LOST HART TRIPLET
Covert Cowboy Soldiers • by Nicole Helm

Zara Hart is desperate to save her innocent sister and needs the help of her ranch's new owner. Undercover navy SEAL Jake Thompson knows he can't get involved in a murder case. But he *won't* let Zara lose her life searching for justice.

#2099 DEAD ON ARRIVAL
Defenders of Battle Mountain • by Nichole Severn

After barely escaping a deadly explosion, Officer Alma Majors has one clue to identify the victim and solve the case: a sliver of bone. But it's going to take more to expose the culprit. Bomb expert Cree Gregson will risk everything to protect his neighbor. Protecting his heart may prove more difficult...

#2100 MONTANA WILDERNESS PURSUIT
STEALTH: Shadow Team • by Danica Winters

Game warden Amber Daniels is tracking a bear on AJ Spade's ranch when he finds a hand wearing a sapphire ring—one he recognizes. A desperate rescue mission makes them learn to trust each other. Now they must work together to save themselves *and* a missing child.

#2101 CAPTURED ON KAUAI
Hawaii CI • by R. Barri Flowers

To discover why a fellow DEA agent was murdered, Dex Adair and his K-9 are undercover at Kauai's most beautiful resort. And when its owner, Katrina Sizemore, receives threatening letters, Dex suspects her husband's recent death might be connected. Is there a conspiracy brewing that will put a stop to Dex and Katrina's irresistible passion—forever?

#2102 ESCAPE FROM ICE MOUNTAIN
by Cassie Miles

When Jordan Reese-Waltham discovers her ex-husband's web of deceit, she must rescue her beloved twin sons. Her destination: ex-lover Blake Delaney's remote mountain retreat. The last thing she expects is for the former marine to appear. But with enemies on their trail, Jordan's reunion with Blake may end as soon as it begins...

Parker pulled his truck and horse trailer to a stop at the side of the ranch house and shifted into Park. Tired, sore from sitting for so long on the three-day trip from Virginia to Whiskey Gulch, Texas, he dreaded stepping out of the truck. When he'd stopped the day before, his leg had given him hell. Hopefully, it wouldn't this time.

Not in front of his old friend and new boss. He could show no weakness.

A nervous whine reminded him that Brutus needed to stretch as well. It had been several hours since their last rest stop. The sleek silver pit bull stood in the passenger seat, his entire body wagging since he didn't have a tail to do the job.

Parker opened the door and slid to the ground, careful to hold on to the door until he was sure his leg wasn't going to buckle.

It held and he opened the door wider.

"Brutus, come," he commanded.

Brutus leaped across the console and stood in the driver's seat, his mouth open, tongue lolling, happy to be there. Happy to be anywhere Parker was.

Ever since Parker had rescued the dog from his previous owner, Brutus had been glued to his side, a constant companion and eager to please him in every way.

Parker wasn't sure who'd rescued who. When he'd found Brutus tied to that tree outside a run-down mobile home starving, without water and in the heat of the summer, he'd known he couldn't leave the animal. He'd stopped his truck, climbed down and limped toward the dog, hoping he wouldn't turn on him and rip him apart.

Brutus had hunkered low to the ground, his head down, his eyes wary. He had scars on his face and body, probably from being beaten. A couple of the scars were round like someone had pressed a lit cigarette into his skin.

Parker had been sick to find the dog so abused. He unclipped the chain from Brutus's neck. Holding on to his collar, he limped with the dog back to the truck.

Brutus's previous owner had yelled from the door. "Hey! Thass my dog!"

Parker helped Brutus into the truck. The animal could barely make it up. He was too light for his breed, all skin and bone.

The owner came down from the trailer and stalked toward Parker barefoot, wearing a dirty, sleeveless shirt and equally dirty, worn jeans.

Parker had shut the truck door and faced the man.

The guy reeked of alcohol as he stopped in front of Parker and pointed at the truck. "I said, thass my dog!"

"Not anymore." Parker leveled a hard look at the man. "He's coming with me."

"The hell he is!" The drunk had lunged for the door.

Parker grabbed his arm, yanked it hard and twisted it up between the man's shoulder blades.

"What the—" he whimpered, standing on his toes to ease the pain. "You got no right to steal a man's dog."

"You had no right to abuse him. Now, I'm taking him, or I'm calling the sheriff to have you arrested for animal cruelty." He ratcheted the arm up a little higher. "Which is it to be?"

The drunk danced on his tiptoes. "All right. Take the damned dog! Can't afford to feed him anyway."

Parker gave the man a shove, pushing him as he released his arm.

The drunk spit on the ground at Parker's feet. "Mutt has no fight in him. The only thing he was good for was a bait dog."

Rage burned through Parker. He swung hard, catching the drunk in the gut.

The man bent over and fell to his knees.

Parker fought the urge to pummel the man into the dirt. He had to tell himself he wasn't worth going to jail over. And that would leave Brutus homeless.

"Touch another dog and I'll be back to finish the job," Parker warned.

The drunk vomited and remained on his knees in the dirt as Parker climbed into the truck and drove away.

Brutus had lain on the passenger seat, staring at him all the way to the veterinarian's office, unsure of Parker, probably wondering if this human would beat him as well.

That had been three months ago, shortly after the removal of Parker's leg cast and his move to the Hearts and Heroes Rehabilitation Ranch.

The therapists at the ranch had been hesitant to bring Brutus on board. They eventually allowed him to move into Parker's cabin after he'd spent a three-week quarantine period with the veterinarian, had all his vaccinations, worm meds and was declared free of fleas.

Parker reached out and scratched Brutus behind the ears. In the three months since he'd rescued the pit bull, the dog had gained twenty pounds. He'd learned to sit, stay, roll over and shake.

More than the tricks, Brutus had helped Parker through therapy. Their walks got longer and longer as both veteran and pit bull recovered their strength.

Parker stepped back from the truck and tapped his leg, the signal for Brutus to heel.

The dog jumped down from the driver's seat and sat at Parker's feet, looking up at him, eager to please.

"Parker Shaw," a voice called out from the porch of the ranch house.

Parker looked up as Trace Travis stepped down and closed the distance between them.

The former Delta Force operator held out his hand. "I'm so glad you finally arrived. I was beginning to worry you had truck or trailer troubles."

Don't miss
Cowboy Justice at Whiskey Gulch *by Elle James,*
available October 2022 wherever
Harlequin Intrigue books and ebooks are sold.

Harlequin.com

HIEXP0822

HARLEQUIN
PLUS

Announcing a **BRAND-NEW**
multimedia subscription service
for romance fans like you!

Read, Watch and Play.

Experience the easiest way to get
the romance content you crave.

Start your **FREE 7 DAY TRIAL** at
<u>www.harlequinplus.com/freetrial</u>.

Love Harlequin romance?

DISCOVER.

Be the first to find out about promotions, news and exclusive content!

Facebook.com/HarlequinBooks

Twitter.com/HarlequinBooks

Instagram.com/HarlequinBooks

Pinterest.com/HarlequinBooks

You Tube YouTube.com/HarlequinBooks

ReaderService.com

EXPLORE.

Sign up for the Harlequin e-newsletter and download a free book from any series at **TryHarlequin.com**

CONNECT.

Join our Harlequin community to share your thoughts and connect with other romance readers!
Facebook.com/groups/HarlequinConnection

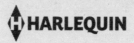